NIKI AGUIRRE

TERMINAL ROMANCE

T0347755

lubin & kleyner
london

Terminal Romance: How to Find Love in Cyberspace

first published as Terminal Romance in eBook format in 2012.
this edition published in 2020 by lubin & kleyner

This book is typeset in Trebuchet MS and
Palatino from Linotype GmbH

lubin & kleyner, london
an imprint of flipped eye publishing
www.flippedeye.net

ISBN: 978-0-9541570-6-7

Supported using public funding by
ARTS COUNCIL
ENGLAND
LOTTERY FUNDED

TERMINAL ROMANCE

How to Find Love in Cyberspace

NIKI AGUIRRE

Back when the Net was still in its infancy, before it became the prison bitch of corporations and porn sites, it was populated by academics, artists and misfits—a community of early settlers who saw their virtual frontier as an expanse of unexplored territory—a place for space cowboys, without laws or sheriffs. And for a while, its denizens felt they could do anything, even walk through walls.

Nina Parks
The Ultimate Guide to Finding Love Online

Contents

CYRANO DE WHATSHISNAME

IT HAD TAKEN Byrd most of the afternoon to prepare for his date. Not that you could tell, thought Frank, as he watched his roommate tackle his wet curls with a broken comb.

"Jesus, did you bathe in Paco Rabanne?"

"I put on a splash, just like you said," said Byrd. "Manny says," and here his roommate made bunny ear quotes, "girls like it when they can smell you.'"

"Manny? Who the hell is Manny?"

"From railwayaficionados."

Frank looked blank.

"Only one of the top five most knowledgeable transport historians in the country."

"Right. So is this *Manny* also an authority on women? Real live ones, not cardboard cut-outs."

"*Frank.*"

"Look, I'm just saying. Should you trust the train guy when it comes to dating? I mean, if you want to know about cabooses you'd ask him."

"What in particular?"

"Nothing, it's an example. Look, girls hate it when you wear too much cologne."

"You think she'll notice?"

Standing six-foot-six with arms so long they practically reached his knobby ankles, Byrd was impossible to miss. In certain circles, he was rumoured to be some kind of Rain-Man savant, able to gut and build computers at the speed of light. He remembered details, (major and minor) of every TV series he'd ever watched, and of course there were his trains and little replica villages he spent hours and hours painstakingly assembling. Byrd knew everything there was to know about the exact shade of red used on a particular model but knew next to nothing about the opposite sex.

Fortunately he had Frank for that.

Frank considered himself a student of life: an analytical observer with street smarts, a renaissance man trapped in a digital age, who gleaned his knowledge from sources other than Youtube or Wikipedia. Frank knew what a real woman smelled like. He didn't have to look it up. For that reason he was perfectly suited to take on the role of World Interpreter to Byrd, advising his roommate on matters of love, fashion and hygiene.

"So what is up with those trousers? You look like a celebrity golfer."

Byrd looked at his legs as if noticing them for the first time. "The label says they're leisurewear and wrinkle-free."

"Two words you should never use when trying to get laid. Did Manny advise you on those too?"

Byrd once told Frank that he couldn't think properly in long trousers. They made him feel restricted. Left to his own devices, Byrd would show up to his date wearing pyjama bottoms or his neon-coloured running shorts.

"Look, stop fussing and sort yourself out."

"I'm trying, but my hair won't cooperate." Byrd slammed down the comb and walked to the kitchen, Frank trailing behind.

"Don't part it like that to the side. You look like Ricky Martin."

"It's hopeless. She's going to hate me."

"Relax, it's just a date. It's not like you're doing open-heart surgery."

"That is a completely illogical comparison, Frank."

"Fine Spock, but just so you know, chicks dig weird guys. That's a fact."

"You don't understand. I want her to think I'm *normal*."

Normal? That was going to be a challenge. Frank sat on the kitchen counter and gnawed on an apple. "She liked you enough to go out with you, so what's the big deal?"

"She liked me *online.*"

"You mean on Facebook?"

Byrd rolled his eyes. "There are other ways to communicate on the Internet other than Facebook, Frank. If you must know, I met her on a forum. She was having problems so I offered a solution."

"I bet you did."

His roommate stared at him blankly. "I just told you I did."

"Byrd, remember what we talked about last time? About you being so literal? Lighten up. It was a joke. See how my voice changed when I said it? You need to work on your sense of humour."

"Sorry, Frank. I'll try harder."

"So anyway, you met on Facebook."

"Forum."

"Same difference."

"No. Completely different."

"Let's agree to disagree. The important thing is that she's cute, right? Can you at least tell me that? Byrd, why are you staring off into the distance?"

"Looks can be highly subjective."

"Are you kidding? Are you freaking kidding me?"

"It's not my fault. She was using an avatar."

"A what?"

"You know, in place of a photo she used a cartoon kitty."

Frank slid off the counter in slow motion. "Tell me something," he said, trying to keep his voice calm. "Who goes out with someone they've never even seen?"

"Lots of people online."

"Yeah and they're all crazy!"

"I'm not crazy," Byrd said softly. "Listen Frank, not everybody is obsessed with appearances. To me looks aren't as important as personality and intelligence, and she has plenty of both to spare. I like her. I would like her even if she had one eye and weighed 500 pounds. Sorry for not providing a photo of her for you to inspect."

Frank winced. He for one would never be convinced that brains and a good personality trumped looks. Even if the girl was Einstein in a skirt, he would never date her unless she was a six. Maybe even a seven. But this wasn't about him. This was Byrd they were talking about. Byrd, who had just challenged him for the first time since they'd met and all because of some pudgy Cyclops he met online.

"Fine. Fine. Let's agree to disagree," Frank said, jumping back on the counter and taking a bite of his apple with relish. "So, this girl with the *personality*, she digs you, right?"

Byrd shrugged.

"Well of course she does. She said yes when you asked her out, right?"

"Not really."

"What do you mean, 'not really'? Do you or don't you have a date, Byrd?"

"That's not how it happened."

Frank sighed. His roommate was beginning to get on his nerves.

"We were on Google Chat and she asked if I wanted to meet up for drinks sometime."

"I don't understand. That's sounds like a date to me."

"I told her no."

Frank's mouth fell open and the piece of apple he'd been chewing fell out.

"Don't look at me like that. I was busy on account of that competition I told you about."

"The replica village?"

"It's been in the pipeline for months. I couldn't just drop everything."

"Let me get this straight. You said no to a real live woman so you could paint trains instead?"

"They're not just trains, Frank. And please don't make fun of me."

"I wasn't. I was being sarcastic," Frank said. "There's a difference."

"Well, don't be insulting or sarcastic."

Byrd may as well have asked Frank to stop breathing.

"So what happened? You said you couldn't go out because you were building miniature storefronts and she said, *oh, that's okay, maybe another time*?"

"No. She was upset. Big time. She wrote an email saying she would no longer talk to me if I had no interest in meeting her. I said I *was* interested. Then she asked if I liked her. I told her 'liking' had nothing to do with being busy. They are two separate concepts."

Frank could feel the big vein in his forehead start to throb. He counted slowly to five. "Then what happened?"

"Well, she accused me of being a coward and told me where I could stuff my concepts. So the next day I agreed to meet her for drinks."

"Then why are you so miserable? The girl sounds like a champ."

"That's exactly it, Frank. If I meet her, she'll see she's right and run away. But if I cancel, she'll never talk to me."

"I don't understand. Don't you want to meet her? Don't you want the date to lead to other things?"

"Such as?"

"Do I have to draw you a diagram?"

"I think it would help."

"Hugging. Kissing. Feeling each other up. For the love of Sutra—SEX, Byrd!"

"Oh," said Byrd. "It's not like that."

"Why the hell not?"

"I wasn't planning on doing it at the first opportunity. It takes time to build up to that kind of thing."

"Forget it. Pull yourself together. This chick sounds like she might be just the thing to get you through your shy phase. How old is she? What does she do for a living?"

"You sound like my mother."

"If I were your mother, I'd dress you better."

"She's a journalist. I think she's in her 30s"

"Older woman? Impressive, Byrd. Those are the sweetest kind. They don't get hung up on the little things like commitment and they're willing to do just about anything for young flesh."

"*Frank.*"

"It's true. Look, I don't care if you're nervous, you're going, my friend, or you'll always be left wondering."

"Wondering what?"

Frank smiled. "Do you know if she's been around? Had lots of boyfriends?"

"I didn't ask. It's a bit personal, don't you think?"

"A man should always know the sexual history of the woman he is interested in. Especially nowadays, when you don't even know what they look like. No reason to be shy. Unless... Byrd, please tell me you didn't meet her on one of those websites. The ones where you need a credit card."

"Of course not."

"Man, I always suspected you had a kinky streak."

"Frank, it's not like that. She's not into that."

"Are you positive? See, that's why you have to straight out ask. Girls can come across all sweet and innocent but give them a webcam and a credit card and they're squirming around like salted slugs."

"That's a horrible thing to say, not to mention deeply offensive. We met on a forum. I told you."

"Okay. I'm just looking out for you."

"By insulting her? If you are going to say mean things Frank, you can just go."

"Sorry. Look, she's into you or she wouldn't have asked you out. Once a woman gets it in her head that she wants something, she won't stop till she gets it. I think you're onto a good thing here. All you have to do is charm the pants off her. Literally. After all, you are wearing my cologne."

Byrd's eyes rolled back in his head. It was something he did when he was nervous.

"Relax, buddy. It's going to be fine."

"I'm not sure, Frank. I think I am going to be sick."

Retching noises came from the bathroom, followed by the sound of running water. Byrd returned in his underwear.

"What happened to your trousers?"

Byrd shrugged as if he didn't understand the question.

"Hey. Stay with me. Take a deep breath. Don't sweat it. What else do you have to wear?" Frank went into Byrd's closet and took inventory. "One pair of tartan trousers, three jogging pants, five assorted running shorts of various colours. Wait, what is this?" He pulled out something from the back of the closet. "Oh and one fucking ugly purple suit."

"What's wrong with it?"

His roommate held up the suit. "Byrd, it looks like it belongs to the Joker. Jesus, don't you have jeans or something?"

"I can't go through with it, Frank. She's going to hate me no matter what I wear. I don't want to go on this stupid date anymore. I like chatting with her. But I don't really care mooning over here over a candlelit dinner. I know you think it's strange, but I don't even want to kiss her. I want things to stay the way they are online. Why do we have to complicate it by meeting? I don't think I can take the stress of feeling like this every time I want to see her. I haven't been able to eat all day." Byrd closed the closet and walked back to the kitchen, his bony shoulders slumped in defeat.

"No wonder you're sick," said Frank, pouring his roommate a glass of water. "If you weren't so gigantic you could borrow some of my clothes."

"No thanks. I don't think leather suits me."

Frank snapped his fingers. "Of course. That's it. Byrd, does she know what you look like?"

"I told you, we didn't exchange photos."

"You didn't describe yourself? Tell her how tall you were, that kind of thing?"

"I don't think so. Frank, how is this helping?"

"Hold on. Let me ask you this: say you go out with her tonight and everything goes smoothly. What then?"

"What's the point of the question?"

"Just answer."

"If it went well and that's a big IF of course I'd want to see her again."

Frank grabbed a pencil and started making notes on the back of a takeout menu.

"What are you writing?"

"I'll tell you in a bit." He scribbled for a few seconds and then leapt off the stool. When Frank got excited, he liked to act out his scenes as if he were a television courtroom lawyer.

"Byrd, I'm going to let you in on a little secret. Women are—well, they're not like men. They appreciate a good personality. They want someone who is smart and confident and funny."

Byrd nodded.

"Which is why I have to go on your date instead of you. Wait. Stop breathing like that. You're going to pass out. Hear me out. It's the oldest trick in the book. Cyrano whatshisname. Remember the story? Listen, we could pull it off. Here are the facts as we know them."

Frank indicated each point with a finger. "One. The thought of going on this date makes you sick to your stomach. Two. You don't have anything decent to wear. Three. This is your last chance. If you stand her up she's never going to talk to you again. There is something you have to remember when it comes to women. They can forgive and forget just about anything except if you offend or wound their pride."

"I thought you were helping. Your list doesn't sound very helpful."

"Three," Frank said, ignoring Byrd." I know everything about you, more or less."

"You're on number four."

"Fine. Four. We don't look anything alike but I can easily impersonate you if I have to, Byrd. Come on, it will be hard for me to play you, make no mistake, but I can do it if I have to. I can do it with my eyes closed. Five…"

"Frank, get your numbering right. You're on six."

"Forget the stupid numbers, Byrd. All you need to know is that I'll do a convincing enough job so that she'll like you. Hell, she'll love you. All you have to do is email her when I get back and tell her what a great time you had. She'll want to see you again. I guarantee it."

"What then?"

"I dunno. Haven't thought that far ahead. I know. Tell her you will be out of town for an extended period of time. The great thing is, you can still talk to her wherever you are. It will be like before, but better, as she'll have had a taste of the legendary Byrd, brought to her by yours truly. Understand what I'm saying? You'll get everything you want. And no annoying date. It's perfect."

"It isn't really. There are too many unknown variables."

"Like?"

"How do you know what I will say?"

"Relax. I got that covered. I'm a great observer of character. I'll be you. Well, a better, more sociable you."

"I don't know, Frank."

"Look, do you or don't you want this to work? Cause if you don't, we can drop the whole thing right now. I'm the one going out on a limb here."

Byrd closed his eyes and sat motionless in his chair for such a long time that Frank thought he'd fallen asleep. "Byrd?" he said nudging the chair.

"I'll agree as long as you tell her some good jokes. She said online that she liked my sense of humour."

"Of course she does," Frank smiled at his friend. "I'll make her laugh, don't you worry. I'll make her laugh so hard she'll want to take you home right there and then."

"You mean YOU."

"Not me, as I'll be playing you, doofus. Stop glaring at me. I'm not going to try anything with your girl. Frankie here is off-limits. Besides, I'm not into online chicks. You know that. I like the more outgoing types, if you get my drift."

Byrd nodded and then went into the hallway closet returning with a moth bitten corduroy jacket with suede fringes.

"What in the hell is that?" Frank said shrinking, as his roommate took it off the satin hanger.

"You have to wear it."

"Over my dead body!"

"Frank, you have to," Byrd insisted. "I told her I'd be wearing it. So she could recognize me. Here, put it on."

"It doesn't fit. The arms are too big."

"Button it up and roll up the sleeves. See? Now you look distinguished. Like a professor."

"You think?" Frank surveyed his profile in the hallway mirror. The jacket added on at least 20 pounds to his frame. It made him look like a 70s TV cop, but not the 'bad' cop of the partnership – the deranged hippy dippy one. He was going out on a ledge for Byrd. He hoped his friend had the good sense to appreciate it.

"Just promise you won't lie to her, Byrd said, his worried eyes meeting Frank's in the mirror. "Don't make me out to be something I'm not. I know I'm not the smoothest guy…"

"Don't worry, man. I got this."

"Okay. Get going or you'll be late. One of the things she's dislikes most is people who are never on time."

"Hey, don't sweat it," Frank said, getting into his good cop role. "I'm in charge. Now hand over me some of that cologne."

***

It took Frank twenty minutes to find the Bluesky. He consulted Byrd's map, passing the place three times before noticing the tiny sign in the window. He'd wanted to make a smooth impression, but when he walked in his usually immaculate hair was dishevelled.

The place was almost empty. There was one woman sitting by herself at the bar with a notebook. He stood beside her and cleared his throat. She calmly finished writing, capped her pen and put it in her handbag. Only then did she look up.

Frank took in the entire scene in slow motion. The curved lips. The black eyebrows. The hair that swung like some kind of velvet curtain. She was breathtaking. There was no other way to describe her.

"You're late," she said.

"Ugh," said Frank, tongue-tied for the first time in his life. He was unable to speak, unable to think, unable to tear his eyes away from her dress, something shiny and skin-tight he thought only girls in magazines wore.

"Something wrong?"

"Yes. I mean, no. I'm Douglas. Sorry I'm late. I was lost. I walked for ages. You can't really see the bar unless you're looking for it."

"Well, I'm glad you made it. I've been looking forward to meeting you." She placed her perfectly manicured hands on his shoulders and softly kissed him on the cheek, near his lips.

Poor Byrd would have passed out. As it was, Frank's hands were trembling and he didn't trust himself to speak. How was it possible that his geeky friend had managed to pull this prize? On what planet did Byrd get so lucky?

Frank had dated his share of pretty girls. Had never had a problem attracting them. But this one was in a different league.

"So, Douglas, tell me something about yourself. Something I don't already know."

Frank tried to think of something clever. Get hold of yourself. Say something smart. Come on. This is just another chick. Woo her with your charm.

"You were so chatty online," she said. "Am I making you nervous?"

"A bit," croaked Frank.

"Well, relax. I don't bite. Not on the first date anyway. What do you like to do for fun?"

"I like running," he finally said. "And computers. I like computers. A lot." Oh God. He was coming off like a nerd.

Frank wished more than anything that he could be himself. That had to be it. Acting like Byrd was actually turning him into Byrd. He wanted so badly to tell her the truth: that her original date was indisposed and he was sent in his stead. The night could turn out to be interesting, but only if he could be Frank, not some antisocial geek who knew nothing about women. As Frank he would totally rock her world.

She was looking at him with those piercing green eyes again, making him feel as if she were searching for the place where he kept all his secrets.

"Is there something wrong? Don't you like me?"

Like her? If he didn't know better he'd think he was falling in love.

"Douglas, it's me. We've been talking for weeks. Please don't be nervous. Besides, remember what we talked about the other night? I know you're not as shy as you're pretending to be." She looked at him and bit her bottom lip.

Frank took a sip of his drink, desperately trying to project an aura of cool. How not shy had Byrd been? What had he said to this beautiful girl to make her sit here flirting with him, instead of laughing in his face?

"You have no idea how much you've entertained me with your stories. Especially about that weird guy you live with, the one with the hair? Does he really refer to himself as a 'Student of Life'?"

"What's wrong with his hair?" Frank asked stiffly.

She laughed and ordered two more drinks. "See? That's what I mean. Just when I think I have you pegged, you come out with the most subversive humour."

Frank had no idea what she was talking about but he had urge to go home, grab his roommate by the scrawny neck and knock him around the room. Here he was doing his best to help out, and all along the lanky bastard and his girlfriend were taking at his appearance. Friendship obviously meant nothing to some people.

"You know, I didn't expect you to look the way you do," she said, staring at him over the rim of her glass.

"What do you mean?"

"I imagined you a lot taller. Taller but nowhere near as handsome." She pressed her knee against his thigh. "So tell me, Douglas. What do you like to do for fun?"

"Fun?" his voice came out as a croak.

"Yeah, *fun*. You've heard of it?"

Finally, here was something Frank understood. He knew how to show a girl a good time without having to resort to cheap jokes. He'd drive her up to the woods to one of those swanky cabins and they'd spend the weekend drinking wine and lounging around on a white fur rug shaped like a bear, naked in front of the fireplace—very, very naked—while Byrd licked his wounds in the kitchen of their apartment, cursing himself for ever making fun of him.

"Excuse me, did you say *bear*, Douglas?" She was looking over his shoulder at a man who had just entered the Bluesky. A tall man wearing a fedora.

The idiot. The stupid gigantic idiot. He told him to wait at home.

Focus, Frank. What would Byrd do for fun? Play with his train collection? Byrd had over two dozen cardboard boxes full of models. He had been collecting them for years and had patiently explained how each worked and how each door and lever had been faithfully and lovingly replicated. Byrd would have bored his date to death in detail.

In the corner of the bar, Byrd had put down the fedora and was steadying the drinks menu while shoving peanuts into his mouth.

"Cooking. I'm into cooking," Frank said, smiling at her with all his teeth.

"That's funny. I'm sure you told me you didn't know how."

"No, you must have misunderstood. I'm definitely into food. In fact, why don't we get out of here and go somewhere quiet for dinner. I know the perfect place. What do you say?"

Good job, Frank. That's more like it. Decisive. Girls liked it when you were decisive.

But his date wasn't listening. She was looking over at the other side of the bar were Byrd was choking, the bartender coming over with a glass of water. As usual his roommate was displaying a complete lack of common sense. Had he forgotten he had a peanut allergy?

"Idiot," he said.

"Excuse me?"

"Not you," said Frank, jumping and in the process, spilling his drink over his date and on Doug's suede jacket. From the other side of the room came a noise that sounded like the bark of a seal.

"I'm so sorry," said Frank. "I'm a clumsy oaf."

"Nice going," said the bartender, after she'd gone to the ladies room to repair the damage.

Frank pointed at their empty glasses. "Can you get another one of whatever she was drinking?"

"Gin or vodka?"

"Gin or vodka what?"

"Martini? Don't you know what kind of martini she drinks?"

"How the hell am I supposed to know, buddy? You're the expert."

"Pardon?"

"I said, make whatever you made for her before." Frank stared him down until the bartender disappeared around the back. The nerve of the guy. How should he know what went in the drinks? At his job, he knew exactly what to do if there was a problem with the toner, or a paper jam. But then not everyone was as good at problem solving as he was. That's where Frank differed from guys like Byrd and Manny. Byrd needed an instruction manual to do anything. Frank relied on his smarts.

He wiped his jacket with a cocktail napkin and went over to Doug who was pretending to study the menu.

"What are you doing?"

"What are *you* doing? You're ruining everything, Frank."

"I'm fine. Listen, you can't stay here, you're going to blow my cover. I have this under control. Go home."

"No."

"Go HOME."

"I wanted to see how you were getting on. You are in serious trouble. I'm staying here."

"Then I'm walking. You can take over if you want."

There was no way Frank was leaving now. He was just starting to get the girl to like him. He wasn't giving her to Byrd now.

"If you don't go, I'll tell her the truth. And you can explain why you lied." He stared Byrd straight in the eyes.

"Fine. You're right, but I wasn't spying. I was just checking, in case you needed my help."

"I have it covered."

"You sure? From here it looks like total date fail. And what happened to my jacket? That was my dad's, Frank."

"Be quiet. She's coming back."

"What were you doing with my glass?" she said, sitting down.

"I was wondering what was in it, that's all. When Bond says 'shaken not stirred' he doesn't specify if it's gin or vodka. I'm afraid I'm not much of a cocktail man. Whiskey is my poison."

She arched an eyebrow. "You told me chocolate milkshake was your poison. You don't drink alcohol, remember?"

"I don't usually. But on special occasions, like today, I like to imbibe."

"Imbibe, huh?"

He took a sip and smiled. Trust her to be impressed by his vocabulary. Sophisticated women, common ones—they were all the same—they wanted a guy who knew what he was doing. Beneath her veneer of cool, this girl wasn't so different from Bette and long-legged Martha. Women were always falling for Frank. He bet himself that once this one got a taste of him, she would lose her mind. That's what women craved. A man who knew how to take control.

"Baby, is your dress OK? I hope it isn't ruined. If it is I'll buy you another."

She shook her head. In the dim light her hair shone by turns electric blue and black. Frank reached out to touch it.

"What are you doing?" She pulled back.

"You have such pretty hair."

"I don't like people touching me." She enunciated each word carefully, her voice like flint.

"This place is dead. What do you say we go somewhere with a little more action? You like dancing?"

"We talked about it," she said quietly.

"Dancing?"

"We talked about perception and honesty. I told you how I felt. I thought we were on the same page, Douglas."

"What do you mean? I'm being honest. I'm really into you."

"Get your hand off my knee. I don't like it when strangers do that."

"I'm not a stranger, babe. I'm your date."

The smile she'd been giving him all night turned to ice.

"Hey, what's wrong? Ouch! What did I do?"

"Touch me again and you are going to lose a finger."

"Sorry. I don't know what came over me. I'm not myself tonight."

"Yeah? That's the first honest thing you've said."

"I don't understand."

"Do you think I was born yesterday?"

Frank took a gulp of his whiskey, resisting the urge to point to the man sitting a few feet away. Him. It was all Byrd's fault.

The bartender came over. "Hey, is this guy giving you trouble?"

"I'm fine, Rob. It's okay."

Rob? She knew the bartender by name? Where did Byrd find this woman?

"Look, I know you're not Douglas, so stop pretending. Who are you?"

"Douglas. I'm Doug."

She crossed her arms.

"Fine. You got me. I'm his roommate Frank."

"The weird guy? What are you doing here? Didn't Douglas want to meet me?"

"He was worried you wouldn't like him. He sent me instead."

"So you thought you'd pull one over on me?"

Frank paused. It wasn't in his nature to bite the bullet but maybe confession would change her mind. "I wanted to help. It wasn't Doug's fault. I put him up to it. Blame me if you're going to blame anyone."

"No problem," she said, standing up and walking to the other side of the bar. "So, are you my real date?"

Before Byrd had a chance to answer, she leaned in, wrapped her arms around his neck and laid a long slow kiss on his surprised lips.

It lasted forever. Frank thought he'd grow old watching that kiss—a kiss that by all rights belonged to him. Why was Byrd was getting all the glory? It wasn't fair. He was the one who had done all the hard work.

"Next time, think twice before you pull a stunt like that," she said to Byrd. "This isn't some dumb film." She wiped her lips with the back of her hand and walked over to Frank.

Here it was. He should have never doubted his power. Women found him irresistible. They always had. That's where he and Byrd were like day and night or chalk and cheese, whatever the hell that meant. Byrd had to try hard to keep his head above water, but Frank understood these things instinctively. He closed his eyes and waited.

"As for you. I don't even have words for you. You blew it for your friend. He was doing fine on his own before you stepped in to help."

She took one last sip of her drink and picked up her purse. "Fucking amateurs," she said, stepping out into the night.

MARTIN: MAN OR MYTH

THE DAY THEY moved in together, Martin lifted up Jillian Jones with great difficulty and carried her over the threshold of his apartment. Jillian, four and a half inches taller than her boyfriend, lay prone in his arms, her limbs pulled toward her like a trussed turkey.

"Don't do that," gasped Martin. "It centres all your weight in one place. Put your arms around my neck. Not so tightly, you're choking me."

He heaved her onto his striped couch. "Home sweet home," he said, shoving a box of DVDs out of the way. "So, what did you think of my romantic gesture? I know how you women go weak at the knees for that kind of stuff."

Jillian who actually abhorred that kind of stuff, didn't bother correcting her boyfriend. How could it be that Martin, a film buff, had not noticed how she flinched when confronted with lengthy make-out scenes and clichéd declarations? Even scenes heavy with expectation made her squirm. She was much more comfortable with books, which dealt with relationships more elegantly, diplomatically and with a tenth of the fanfare. Despite all this, Martin insisted on believing she was a closet romantic.

Jillian took in her new surroundings. Martin's apartment (hers now too, she corrected herself) was cluttered with cardboard boxes and bubble wrap. The studio apartment, cosy before, was borderline claustrophobic. The bathroom had one window the size of a postage stamp and no available shelf space. She was forced to stow her family-sized conditioner and mouthwash in her suitcase. And the compact kitchen with its tiny pots and pans made her feel like Gulliver invading Lilliput.

"The problem is you have too much stuff," said Martin, philosophically.

They had agreed to move in together over email, enumerating the benefits and convenience of cohabitation. 1. Martin's apartment was five minutes away from Jillian's university. 2. Jillian's lease was almost up and she had to hunt for a new place anyway. 3. Martin's place was big enough for the both of them.

Their four-month virtual courtship had been ideal. Compatible in most matters, reality had only reared its ugly head when they were assembling the Ikea bookshelf Jillian purchased. After 24 hours it remained disassembled in the living room.

"Tell me again why you need a new shelf?" said Martin, giving up on the directions and stretching out on the floor.

"Because yours is currently full of toys."

"Not *toys*. Action figures," he said.

"Martin, I need a place to put my books."

"Fine. You take the shelves. I'll keep my stuff in the storage area."

"You mean the area currently holding the computer parts? And anyway, it's not like you have a lot of books."

"What do you mean?" He pointed at the shelves. "What did you call those?"

"Come on Martin, comics don't count."

"Graphic novels, Jillian. *Award-winning* books. They most definitely count. They absolutely count."

When they'd first met, he'd written how he was a fellow lover of literature. He even quoted that Mark Strand poem she liked so much, the one about devouring books. Jillian printed out Martin's email and carried it around with her, re-reading it over and over so many times that it finally tore. She taped up the corners, transparent with wear and still kept it in her wallet, even though it was impossible to read now.

Where were those wonderful books Martin had talked about? Where were the collections of poetry? The vintage Salinger? Jillian was beginning to think he'd made it up.

"I sold them on eBay," Martin said. "The rest I donated when you agreed to move in. We needed the room." He stood up, his dark hair rumpled. "Why do you need so many books anyway? Haven't you read them already?"

Jillian was so speechless she had no reply.

In the films Martin liked to watch, couples moved in together to a soundtrack of 80s pop. The struggles, if any, involved larger-than-average mattresses or hideous lamps that clashed with the perfect décor. Couples on celluloid never fought over bookshelves full of Star Wars figures or Swedish furniture instructions. They were never shown walking around the apartment in dazed, zombie-like confusion, trying to fit cosmetics into impossible bathrooms or tripping over cardboard boxes.

How had they arrived so quickly at this juncture, when all they had wanted was to be together?

"How are things with Martin?" asked Aurora Andorra, Jillian's great aunt. They were in the garden, Aurora wearing a large sunhat with dangling cherries that trembled whenever she shook her head.

"Fine, I guess. Things are still a little awkward. Online it was easier between us."

"That's because he's getting the milk for free now. Men change when you shack up," said Lucinda, older than her sister by ten minutes and the dark to Aurora's light. Dressed in black lace gloves and a taffeta gown, she'd been wearing mourning garb for the past thirty years, even though her husband was not technically dead. After catching him with another woman, Lucinda tried to bash Uncle Edward's head in with the iron skillet given to her as a wedding present. Rumour had it that when Edward returned to the house to ask for his wife's forgiveness, Lucinda pretended she couldn't hear him, as he was a ghost.

Jillian didn't know what she would do if Martin left her for someone else, but her response most likely would not involve cooking implements. She and Martin had talked about it, the way they had talked about so many things, with the calm assurance of couples that knew, even while discussing the most hypothetical breakup scenarios, that it could never happen to them. They were safe in the virtual cocoon they had built for themselves, reassuring one another that if their relationship didn't work, they would calmly (and without bitterness) go their separate ways.

The truth was that Jillian didn't feel jealously or anguish when she thought of Martin with another woman. She felt annoyed, like when he forgot to buy the toilet paper or when he stuffed the utility bills in the cutlery drawer.

"Nowadays no one is interested in buying or even selling the entire cow, Auntie. I know it's hard for you to understand. You come from a generation raised to respect the sanctity of marriage. But we don't have to tolerate the kind of peccadilloes that got you into trouble all those years ago. Women have options now."

"Until he died, your Uncle was a good man, Lucinda said, waving the knife with which she was cutting lemons.

"Dead is dead," agreed Aurora. "Lucy, if you cut those any thinner they're going to disintegrate.

"So nowadays you have guarantees that you won't get hurt if Martin decides to play the field?" asked Lucinda.

Jillian giggled. "No guarantees. Just options. Besides, Martin isn't the kind to cheat."

"And how would you know? You met him in your computer!"

"On, not in, Auntie."

"It doesn't matter where they met," Aurora smiled at her sister. "The important thing is that they are in love."

"Well, I don't know if I'd call it that."

"But you live together." Both aunts turned to stare at their niece.

"It is too early to tell what will come of it. Maybe it's more than a casual thing. Maybe we're just making time. See? That's the beauty of it. We can take what we want and leave the parts we don't like behind. No need for anyone to get upset if it doesn't work out."

"Well I've never heard such rot," Lucinda, placing the mangled lemons on a plate.

"Calm down, Lucy, you're going to give yourself hives."

"Well Aurie, it shows an appalling lack of commitment on behalf of young folks these days. Jillian, if you are serious about this man you can't just go around the table selecting the good bits like you are at a senior buffet."

"If she does that, she'll starve," quipped Aurora. "Now, all this talk of food is making me hungry. Who's ready to eat?" she said, passing around plates.

"I didn't mean to upset you Aunties. It wasn't my intention," said Jillian. "I know you mean well, but very little in this day and age, especially romance, is do or die. People do the best they can with what they have, but we don't believe anything is permanent or absolute. We're not built for longevity." She picked up her fork. "This is really delicious potato salad, by the way.

The sun shone on the three ladies as they sat in the garden eating their lunch.

"So, what's Martin like in the sack? That's what I want to know."

"Lucinda Patricia Andorra!" said her sister, the cherries dancing on her head.

"What? Don't pretend you aren't curious, Aurie. Come on Jillian, dish the details."

"Lucy, let her be. Look how the poor thing is blushing."

"*Exactly.* She may pretend she and her kind are open-minded and blasé about their entanglements, but scratch under the surface and they're a conservative bunch at heart. At least our generation knew how to appreciate a good romp when we came across it," Auntie Lucinda said, happily biting into her sandwich.

The summer before Jillian moved in with Martin, she worked as an intern for a consulting firm. During a team-building workshop, the entire office had to take part in a task the mediator called 'trust participation circle'. But when it came time for Jillian to close her eyes and fall into the waiting arms of her teammates, she couldn't do it.

Living with Martin was like that, but without the cheering and encouragement.

"You have to learn to trust me, Jillian," he kept saying. Even as she discovered new things about her boyfriend that he had never bothered mentioning online. Such as how many hours he truly spent playing computer games or his obsession with sunflower seeds. He would go through entire bags, leaving them between the pages of his comic books so they spilled onto the table and floor. There were husks inside dirty plates and glasses, left on windowsills and cupboards. She even found them in the shower. It got to the point where Jillian would walk around the apartment, eyes unfocused; she wouldn't see the disgusting little grey carcasses.

Living with Martin was like living with an unemployed person. Even though he was gainfully employed as a freelancer, she never saw him do any work. They never went out. Never did anything. Jillian observed him from the kitchen-slash-makeshift office, as night after night, her boyfriend sat slumped on the couch, a can of soda in one hand and a game controller in the other.

"Why don't you ever take any photographs?" Jillian asked, pointing at Martin's unused camera equipment.

"Huh?" he said, not even bothering to turn his head from his game.

"I thought photographers were obsessed with snapping the world around them."

"Mmh. Not all the time." Martin waved his hand dismissively. "It may not look like it to you, but I'm working on something important right now. I'm not sitting around idly, you know."

A few days later when he left the apartment, Jillian peeked into Martin's notebook and found a sketch called 'Man or Myth'. It was dated three months before they'd met. In the margins, he had scribbled a line about desensitized man and his subjection to technological culture, followed by a series of esoteric doodles. Except for the sketches, the notebook was empty. Almost a year and he hadn't worked on anything.

"I'll throw myself into the project once you start classes again," he told her.

"Martin, classes started three weeks ago. Haven't you noticed?"

He looked at her with his hooded, bloodshot eyes. Martin had the eyes of a man who had never had a good night's sleep in his life. He was twenty-seven but he had the eyes of a forty-four year old man. Had he always looked like that? She couldn't remember. The photos he had sent her over email were artfully shot. Angles. Limbs. Profiles. Black and whites of a contemplative man, head bowed. He should have sent her a more realistic photo: Martin wearing sweatpants, his dirty feet on a coffee table amid a sea of sunflower seeds.

"Maybe you should give the games a rest for a bit," Jillian said, sitting beside him on the couch. He continued playing, barely registering her presence. She wanted him to hold her and talk to her the way he used to. Over chat he had seemed so sure of himself. The kind of man who knew what he wanted; who had purpose and ambition. In person, Martin moved through life in a catatonic state. He barely ate, never slept and wasn't interested in sex or any type of physicality with her. He had written dozens of emails, detailing, promising, luring her with the things he would do if only she were there beside him.

"I'm here now," she said, wanting to throw his controller across the room and smashing it into a million pieces. "I'm here is this room right now and you won't even look at me."

"Sorry Jilly, did you say something?"

Transitioning from an online relationship was simply a matter of managing expectations, Jillian told herself, sounding like speaker at a corporate seminar. While she had imagined them going to arty films and afterward to all-night cafes where they would sit for hours discussing lighting and cinematography, their reality was strikingly different. The one time she lured Martin to an all-night showing of Blade Runner, he fell asleep in the cinema, waking only when the credits were rolling.

Jillian wanted museums, impromptu picnics, Shakespeare in the Park. She wanted Martin to accompany her to bookstores, poetry readings and art exhibits, sipping white wine and holding hands as they shared insider jokes. The image of Martin that she spent countless evenings pining for was that of a turtleneck wearing artist—someone who would explain his use of shadow while simultaneously brushing his fingertips across her cheeks and commenting on the beauty of her cheekbones. Real Martin hated turtlenecks and had no interest in explaining his photographs.

Maybe he had been right about her all along. Maybe she *was* a closet romantic. Jillian stared at Martin's profile. Could it be that he genuinely recognised and appreciated her for who she really was, when all along she'd been frustrated by his persona?

She placed her hand on Martin's thigh. He ignored it, continuing to shoot at monsters. She placed her hand higher on his thigh, tracing a figure-eight pattern round and round, until he finally put down the controller.

"Jillian," he said, looking sheepish. "I'm bushed. Maybe tomorrow when I'm not so tired."

But the next day when she returned from classes, he was dressed and waiting to take her to the opening of a department store where he purchased a new game console. Martin, more excited than Jillian had ever seen him, danced up and down the aisles like a child. At the register, he asked if he could put the purchase on her credit card.

"I'll pay you back my half next month."

"Half?"

"We agreed to split all purchases down the middle, remember?"

"I thought that meant bills and rent."

"Well I chipped in for the bookshelf, so it's only fair," Martin said.

"Classic virtual-goggles scenario," said Nina Parks, who had known Jillian during her graduate days.

"Tell me about it," said Jillian, as she held the phone in the crook of her neck as she boiled a pack of noodles. "I thought I'd outgrown the need for fantasy, but look at me—living with a guy just because he liked the same poem I did. Want to know the saddest thing? I suspect he's never even read the damn poem."

"You need to be more assertive," said Nina. "Don't get hung-up over what doesn't work. You saw something in him, right? Reignite the spark you had online. Sometimes you have to take more of an initiative with shy guys."

"Martin isn't shy. He's lazy."

"So work with it. Just don't give up until you're absolutely sure he's a lost cause."

"God, you sound like my 86 year old aunt."

"I thought you wanted my advice, Jillian."

"I do but 'sparking' is difficult when I can't even get my boyfriend's attention."

"What's he doing at the moment?"

Jillian looked over at Martin, who was sitting in front of the television. "He's killing zombies."

"Sure he's not eavesdropping on our conversation?"

"Martin," Jillian called out. "I spent my half of the rent on books. They're being delivered tomorrow. You're going to have to get rid of your Xbox." She waited for a few minutes. "See?" she said to Nina. "I told you he wasn't listening."

"Number one, Jones. Stop moping," said her friend. "Walk around naked. Give him a lap dance. Put on your sexy underwear and stand in front of that television until he looks at you."

Easy for *her* to say, Nina was the 'Internet Relationship Guru', writing books about the dangers of filling in empty spaces. "That's what newbies do when they go online looking for romance, Jillian. They take bits and pieces from conversations and quilt them together. They make Frankenstein personas that no one can live up to. They aren't imaginary but they aren't exactly real either."

"I know all that," said Jillian under her breath. "I'm the one who taught you to chat all those years ago. Or have you forgotten?"

"Well then, quit acting like a rookie, Jones. Face it. You got complacent. You let loneliness and a stupid poem get in the way of common sense. Now stop whining and get out there and do something. You're bringing me down," said Nina.

"Nina Parks is full of it," said Jillian. "Excuse my language, Aunties. She means well but you can't sort out your relationship using someone else's blueprint. What works for her won't necessarily work for me. She should tell people the truth." Jillian picked up an apple from the fruit bowl.

"Don't eat that dear, it's wax," said Aurora.

"This is what I was trying to say the last time. Nothing lasts forever. Forever is an illusion. We want to be loved and understood but ultimately we know we're doomed, so we cling and get disillusioned. It makes you bitter."

"I beg your pardon," sniffed Lucinda.

"I didn't mean you. Auntie. I just meant that it takes guts to walk away from something that isn't working. You must know that better than anyone."

"It takes guts to stay, too, dear," said Aurora. "Remember that."

"And if that doesn't work you can borrow my skillet," added Lucinda.

"I'm not sure what you want from me," Martin said. "Everything annoys you. You have habits that get on my nerves too. You open the curtains when I'm sleeping, even though I've told you how sensitive my eyes are to light. And you sing, Jillian. ALL the time: when you are writing, when you're cooking. You even sing in bed. It drives me crazy."

"What's wrong with singing?"

"That's another thing I don't get about you. When did you turn into such a neat freak? It's like you are right there with a brush and dustpan every time I turn around. Then there's the food thing," he said.

"What food thing?"

"That crazy thing you do when you separate all your food, Jillian! Jesus, the first time we went out to dinner I barely heard a word you said because I was too busy watching you compartmentalize your food onto different sections of your plate."

Jillian stared at him. "Why didn't you say something?"

"What did you want me to say?" asked Martin. "Why won't you let your broccoli touch the rice, you freak?"

"If you'd said something I could have explained that I prefer things not to overlap on my plate. Otherwise, everything ends up looking and tasting like a big unidentifiable lump. Surely you of all people should understand the importance of aesthetics?"

Martin shook his head.

"So you had unrealistic expectations too. You imagined me to be a woman who never separates her food or who drives you crazy with her singing. You wanted someone who never complains about your gaming and you got me instead."

"Jillian, I know we are fundamentally different but it doesn't change how I feel about you."

"And how is that?" she said, wary of his reply. Would Martin admit that it was a mistake to move in together?

"Online environments are something else, aren't they? If you had told me online about the singing, I would have thought it was really cute. Experiencing it every day is another matter. Reality is fickle." Martin smiled at her.

For a moment, Jillian was reminded of how sweet Martin could be but he quickly put a stop to that.

"You still don't get it, Jillian. Ultimately, the curtains, the freaky food thing, the obsession with neatness, none of it matters. Know why? I don't believe anything in this life happens by accident. Fate," her boyfriend said, hitting the coffee table and scattering a pile of seeds. "You and me are *meant* to be together."

"Martin."

"I know you think all our problems stem from meeting online. But normal dating wouldn't have flagged them up either. I wouldn't know about your impossible no-mess policy and you wouldn't know about my sleeping schedule. Those are the kinds of things you discover about a person when you live together."

"But I feel I don't know a single constant fact about you. Everything is in flux."

"That's the fun part," Martin said, holding Jillian's hand and kissing each finger individually. "Working out the kinks of a relationship is like playing a game. You have to be methodical. You have to be strategic. You have to have a great deal of patience and take the time to really get to know me. Most of all, you have to trust that you made the right choice."

"He is right," said Aurora. "Sometimes you have to jump and hope the other person is there to catch you."

"I'm tired of Martin repeating it like a mantra. '*You need to trust me more, Jillian*'. Trust has nothing to do with it. He picks his ears. He wears dirty socks for days on end, and he spits those disgusting sunflower seeds everywhere."

"That reminds me. Jilly, do you remember Lila's son Frank? Did you know he met the love of his life online after reading that blog written by your friend."

"Nina?" said Jillian in disbelief. She knew that her old friend's blog was popular but people actually got together after taking her advice?

"That's right," said Aurora. "After months of emails, Frank met the girl of his dreams in a deli, you know, the one on 37th street. Not the new one. The other one, the one that makes the crunchy pickles."

"I love their pickles," said Lucinda.

"Next time we visit, I'll have to get you the marinated olives, Jillian. They're spectacular."

"Auntie Aurora, back to the story please."

"She was the most glorious thing Frank had ever laid eyes on."

"Skin like peaches, lips like berries, breasts like mozzarella cheese, you get the picture," interjected Lucinda.

"What does that have to do with Martin?" asked Jillian.

"Patience, dear," said Aurora. "I'm getting to that part. Frank placed his order—lightly toasted bagel with a smear of cream cheese and extra onions. And guess what? It was the exact same thing she was going to order. They knew at that moment that it was meant to be. It was fate bringing them together."

"Because they ordered the same bagel?

"What are the odds?"

"Don't you see?" said Jillian, looking from one aunt to the other. "There is no such thing as fate—just other things masquerading behind the scenes. Frank's eyes were sending out signals: *Here I am. Look at me. I'm so tired of being alone.* Her eyes responded in kind. It wasn't an accident or even destiny that they got together. It was plain, human need. Our notion of romantic love is nothing more than the search for a mate. That grin of hers that set his heart on fire? Nothing more than a well-sharpened tool in her arsenal. I'm not saying she purposely set out to snare him. We're talking about Frank, after all."

Lucinda chortled. "So now you're saying that dating is akin to biological warfare?"

"It is true that a woman's eyes can be as effective as weapons," said Auntie Aurora. "Look at Cleopatra."

"Or Helen of Troy," said Jillian.

"Or Mati Hari," said Lucinda.

"You see, Aunties? Everything has a logical explanation. In Frank's case he was ready to fall in love. A question of being in the right time and place."

Aurora clicked her tongue.

"What's wrong?"

"You keep missing the point, dear, that's what. Forget fate. Forget whether you met him in a deli or on a computer. If you want your relationship with Martin to work, you have to trust in yourself. Having things in common is not everything. It is not a guarantee you will get along."

"My sister is right," said Lucinda. "I met Edward at a dance. We talked for hours. We had so much to say, we couldn't get it out fast enough. I never met anyone I was more in tune with than that man. Even my twin here. He still left. He left me anyway.

"Lucy, don't say that. He passed away, he didn't leave you."

"Let me finish, Aura." Lucinda looked up at Jillian, the dark pupils in her shrunken eyes wide. "Listen. I know Edward didn't pass away. I wanted him dead though. Given the chance, I would probably try to kill him again. I'd marry him all over again too. As terrible as it was finding him in the arms of that other woman, I would still choose him. Not the pain or the desperation. I wouldn't wish that on anybody. Maybe it wasn't fate or destiny that brought us together that night. But it certainly wasn't loneliness. It wasn't desperation. I was a looker in my time. Ask Aurie here. I could have had any man I wanted but I wanted Edward."

Lucinda's fragile lacy hands shook as she reached for her cup of chamomile. "I have no regrets. Even knowing what

I know now, I would still love that rotten, cheating bastard with every ounce of my being. So help me God."

That evening when she went home, Jillian lit three scented candles, stripped to her underwear and attempted a move she'd seen in a Shakira video.

"Not now," Martin said, looking embarrassed. "I want to finish this."

"Finish it later," she said in a throaty voice.

"You are going to dislocate something," he said. "Come on, Jillian. If you want me to stop playing, just ask me to stop playing."

"I can't believe you," she said, still shaking her hips. "You were so into me online. If I had typed out what I was just doing now, you would have gone into overdrive."

"Do I really need to point out that we aren't online anymore?"

"Forget it," she said, snuffing out the candles.

"I don't understand why you are you so upset," he said. "I thought we talked about this. You agree to have any patience. To give me time to find my rhythm. You know what you need?"

"Don't say it. Don't you dare. Actually, you know what? Fuck faith. Fuck you too, Martin."

The next day, Jillian packed her suitcase while Martin slept and arranged her books in boxes to be picked up later. She thought about leaving something significant on the coffee table in sunflower seeds, like MARTIN: MAN OR MYTH with the MAN scratched out but that wasn't her style, so she just wrote YOU OWE ME FOR THE PLAYSTATION.

THE ULTIMATE GUIDE TO
FINDING LOVE ONLINE

FIFTY DATES IN and Nina Parks was exhausted, worn out from taking trains and cabs and buses to spend her evenings with men whose names she couldn't remember the next day. The dates were invariably the same. Over chat and email, the candidates were witty and flirty and eager. In person, they clammed up without as much as a memorable line. Old, tall, young, nerdy, they sat across from her, stony and reticent, monosyllabic, as if they were on an interview instead of a date. If Nina pushed, they stared at her with hostility or confusion, as if she were an alien creature that didn't understand their ways.

"What do you like to do?"

"You know, the usual."

"Would you like another drink?"

Shrug.

"Want to go somewhere else? Bernie's down the street makes a mean thin crust."

"No, thank you."

"No, you don't like pizza? No, you don't like the place?"

Silence.

"So, where do you see yourself in five years?"

The idea had been hers from the start. 365 dates. An entire year of coffees, dinners and drinks with men she met online. Nina would blog about her experiences with the aim of promoting her self-help book: The Ultimate Guide To Finding Love Online.

"No one wants to read another sad little blog about how hard it is to find love on the Internet," said Fallon, one of the few publishers interested enough in listening to her idea. "Besides, the market is saturated with dating books."

"Not as well-researched, as mine. I didn't jump on the virtual wagon overnight, like some of these wannabes. I was writing how-to guides before online dating was even an acceptable term! I've earned my credentials."

"Nina, the Internet doesn't give a damn about your credentials," said Fallon. "It's a pissing contest. It's about who screams the loudest."

"Exactly. That's why I'm proposing a testosterone-fuelled-super-challenge instead. Over the next year, I, Nina Parks, will date a different man for every day of the year. I will go out with lonely hearts, pretenders and misfits in a quest to prove that a good online man is not so hard to find."

"Belle de Jour has already been done," Fallon said, leafing through her appointment book

"Yes, but this isn't about sex. This is about good old-fashioned romance."

"Go on," said the publisher.

"Romance with a twist. An updated fairy tale, if you will—Internet reality complete with ogres, dragons and the obligatory kissing frogs. And all of it: the bad, the ugly, the painfully awkward, will be digested in Technicolor on my blog."

"Remind me again where your book fits in?"

"That's the genius part," said Nina. "I'll give them the blog for free, build up my readership, and sell the dating advice they'll so badly need if they want to find their own prince or princess. It will work. Want to know why?" Nina leaned in. "Because an honest to goodness love story never gets old." She sat back and beamed her most confident smile.

As she left Fallon's office, Nina experienced an intense moment of rage followed by crippling doubt. All those years of hard work--all that effort to write a book and it still wasn't good enough. Rejection followed by feeble nibbles followed by more rejection, until she'd come up with her hook and suddenly they were interested. It angered her that even now she had to play games to get the attention of those that ruled the publishing world. Nina took a deep breath and then another one for good measure. By the time she hit the ground floor she was composed again. Getting her book out there was what really mattered. What was a year of her life in exchange for the privilege? Nina stepped out of the building, put on her sunglasses and decided to walk the five miles home.

Two days later, Fallon called to tell her the news. They wanted the book. They wanted the blog. They wanted everything.

Candidate Number 1 claimed to be a black belt in karate. He showed up to dinner wearing a turtleneck, striped trousers and a large medallion that looked like a prop out of *Enter the Dragon*. He kept referring to his physical 'moves', as they sat eating Chinese dumplings. Nina was tempted to ask whether he really had studied martial arts or if he had gained his knowledge solely from playing Mortal Kombat. He was one of the clumsiest, most ungraceful men Nina had ever encountered, almost poking her eye out with his chopsticks and later, dropping his noodles on her lap, as he illustrated the proper way to surprise an opponent. When the time came to say goodbye, he leaned in to kiss her, lost his balance and smacked his head on the edge of table.

Candidate Number 12 spent most of their date hiding behind a large terracotta plant. Nina spotted him as soon as she entered the restaurants, but pretended she couldn't see him and engrossed herself in the menu.

"You my date?" he asked, finally approaching their table. He didn't wait for Nina to reply. He took a handkerchief from his pocket and carefully wiped the chair, his glass and the silverware before sitting down. "Germs," he informed her in a nasally voice. He spent the rest of the time talking about contagious diseases, both established and imaginary. Shortly before the main course arrived, he scuttled off to the bathroom. Nina had the uncomfortable sensation she was being watched but could not confront him, as her date never returned.

Candidate 27 barely said anything during dinner. "Are you okay?" Nina asked, when he suddenly crumpled over, assuming the duck and cover position. "Are you feeling sick? Want me to call anyone?" She asked, putting her hand on his shoulder, but he just curled himself into a tighter ball. "Better let him be," said the waiter. "I'll keep an eye on him." A concerned Nina waited outside restaurant, only to see Number 27 emerge a few minutes later, a mobile phone glued to his ear. Apparently the 'stunner' he'd been out with was crazy gaga for him, forcing him to play dead to get rid of her. The stunner upon hearing this had to restrain herself from pushing him in front of a bus, as her oblivious date passed her on the street.

On paper Candidate 49 was impeccable, describing himself as a man with eclectic tastes, into architecture, street art, and urban renewal. Nina was looking forward to their date, but he was in a dark mood as he stumbled into the Bluesky Bar twenty-three minutes late.

"I must have passed this place ten times. I thought it was condemned," he said, looking around at the faded carpets and discoloured curtains. "Good Lord, it should be."

"The Bluesky is a landmark," said Nina, raising one eyebrow.

"It smells like old dog farts," Candidate 49 insisted.

"It oozes character," said Nina. "I thought with your pedigree you'd appreciate a bit of history."

"History, yes. Dives, not so much."

"Well you wouldn't look too great either if you'd been around for 100 years," she said, trying to fight the impulse to walk out on this charlatan who didn't know the first thing about anything. He was a pretender. Not even a good one at that.

"With all the decent bars in the city, why did you pick this one? It can't be the ambience or the romantic mood lighting or the clientele. Jesus, look at all those sad freaks. Tom Waits would have no problem writing about this place."

Nina slowly counted to ten. "You really want to know?"

"Yeah," I do," he said, grabbing a handful of peanuts from the bar.

Nina waited until they were in his mouth. "I wouldn't eat those if I were you. Look, the Bluesky may be old and decrepit but this bar is the genuine article, full of intrigue and secrets it's kept for generations. See all those pictures on the walls of the infamous characters: Gangsters, molls, politicians, writers, starlets, streetwalkers, they all sat in the very spot you are sitting in."

Her date jumped up from his stool. "Eww. I think I'll stand if you don't mind."

"Be my guest," said Nina, her green eyes glittering.

"OKAY, so it had its share celebrities in its heyday--it's still a relic and should be put out of its misery. Some things shouldn't exist just because *some* people have a soft spot for old smelly buildings. Now can we go please someplace else?"

"Tell you what," said Nina. "There's a nice modern wine bar down the road called Lou-Lou's. Meet you there after I finish my drink."

"You sure?" Number 49 said, already slipping on his jacket. "Listen, don't be too long. We wasted enough time here and there are so many things I want to talk to you about."

"Give me another and don't be stingy with the olives," Nina said to the bartender.

"Here you go. I made it a double."

"Thanks, Rob," said Nina.

"May I ask you something?" he said, setting down her drink. "How does someone like you find so many losers?"

"He wasn't so bad. You should see some of the others I've been out with."

"Jagoffs, Knuckledraggers, Scumwads? Thanks, I've met your suitors. You bring most of them here. Probably to scare them away."

Nina smiled and sipped her martini. "Hey, if they can't see the charm of this place, that's their problem."

"To each his own," Rob shrugged philosophically.

Nina waited until the bartender disappeared before opening her notebook. She kept a foldout list for each candidate, rating them on a complicated system of plusses and minuses. Before each date, the candidate received points for attributes evidenced in chat or email: good spelling for example, or a talent for storytelling. During the date, this net was added to or subtracted from depending on how well the characteristics matched up with previous specs.

Nina would excuse herself to powder her nose, but it was really to adjust the stats in her notebook in private, until the figures balanced. In this instance, Nina had given Candidate 49 pre-points for intelligence and sense of humour. He also received points for hygiene, dress sense, and overall physical presentation, which he had not exaggerated. From this sum, Nina subtracted tardiness (-2), lack of witty repartee (-3), and stupidity (-5), putting his total in the negative. Satisfied, she folded up 49's list and put the notebook back in her bag. Without a checklist, there was no way to objectively evaluate the dates. No matter how graceful and charming the candidate had been post-meet, what counted, as in most things in life, was the face-to-face.

Before embarking on the 365-date challenge, Nina imagined that meeting men online and having drinks with them afterward would be interesting, perhaps even fun. Despite what she told Fallon, she had no intention of falling in love. Romance was another matter. But while she may have once been partial to antisocial guys with limited social graces, after almost 50 dates, Nina was growing weary. She was no longer sure if there really was a difference between the quiet shy type and the more outspoken variety of male with their macho come-on lines. At least with the macho man you knew where you stood.

"Be warned," she wrote later in her blog. "Beneath the awkward wrapping of the geek, beats the stealthy heart of a desperate hunter."

"So," Rob said, coming over to refill her glass again. "What happens when you get tired of dating losers? Does a regular guy even stand a chance with you?"

"I don't know," said Nina. "After 300 more dates I'll let you know."

"Why 300? I don't understand."

"Never mind. In any case, I'm currently off romance, but I appreciate the drink."

By the time Candidate Number 125 came along, Nina wasn't even taking copious notes anymore. Her notebook pages were split into two-column headings: Yes and No. Despite online proclamations of being an adrenaline junky, Number 125 turned out to be the kind of guy who had difficulty climbing a set of stairs, much less a mountain. He arrived at the Bluesky, red-faced, out of breath, the back of his shirt damp with sweat. Nina handed him a cocktail napkin, which he used to wipe his forehead until it fell into shreds. While he composed himself, Nina ordered another drink. Rob silently poured her one and then gave a brief now toward her date and rolled his eyes. Nina could feel a migraine forming at the base of her neck. Before her 365-date challenge, she rarely suffered from anything. Now she was finding it hard to get out of bed, plagued by insomnia, cramps, muscle aches and dizziness. Most nights, Nina went home and paced around her living room sleepless and feverish, swigging directly from a wine bottle and wondering how she could continue with her challenge. She had no idea the dates would make her so bone-tired and suck the life from her so she had no energy, even for the things she loved.

"Stop it," she admonished herself. Her date was no Bear Grylls, that was obvious, but at least he hadn't stood her up like her last two candidates. Besides, there were worse things than a bad date: a root canal, for example, or a tax audit. Except that the option of a quiet evening at home surrounded by shoeboxes of receipts sounded dreamy in comparison to an evening with a guy who was slurping his soft drink so loudly, even though there was nothing left in his glass but ice.

Nonplussed, Nina sat back in her chair and asked Number 125, online nickname, the 'Thrillseeker' whether climbers packed rolls of toilet paper with the pulleys and safety equipment or if they carried it on their person, in case of emergencies. It was a silly question, but she needed a conversation starter.

Her dated stared back blankly.

"Fine. Forget the toilet paper," she said. "What kind of boots would you recommend for a climbing newbie like me?"

Candidate 125 took his iPhone out of his front pocket and tapped away furiously for a few seconds before shoving it in Nina's face. On the screen was an image of a pair of worn hiking boots that he claimed were his own. He then showed her a series of photographs of his climbs, ending with one of him placing a flag on the summit of an impossible looking mountain. Nina squinted at the pictures and nodded happily. She couldn't make out the face but that didn't change the fact that she was impressed with her date's skilful use of Photoshop. A writer once advised: always know what kind of shoes your character wears. 125 seemed to have taken that verbatim. He spent the next hour telling her about his hair-raising adventures, making climbing Everest look like a nature trip for the elderly.

Nina felt herself relaxing for the first time in months. This is what she had expected from her blind dates—a seamless transition from the online experience to the face-to-face encounter. It wasn't about the exaggerations and deceptions her dates meted out. It was about follow through. And this guy: overweight, clumsy, unsporty, had made yarn-spinning into an extreme sport. He was the Shaun White of the Internet. At one point he even asked Rob for some rope to demonstrate his skill with sea-faring knots.

Nina, better than most, understood the need for reinvention. That was the thing she loved most about meeting people online—the limitless options, the belief that you could be anyone, do anything. But once they met in person, the men lost their glitz and glamour. They become ordinary and dull, let down by unrealistic expectations of themselves. Nina tried to tell them that it was okay. That she was prepared to accept they had climbed Kilimanjaro. All they had to do was keep spinning and she would happily go along with whatever they said: snowboard champ, rocket science wiz, World of Warcraft nerd.

When Candidate 125 excused himself to go to the bathroom, Nina pulled out her notebook and started her point system anew. It was what the books called a 'turning point'. If there was one of these guys were every 50, she reasoned, then all wasn't lost.

Later, she wrote: It doesn't matter if I don't know the real identity of the man behind the mask. If a superhero returns from the bathroom with a piece of toilet paper stuck to the bottom of his shoe, does that make him less of a superhero? She called this the Slug vs Superman conundrum and told her readers that there was a difference in how you saw yourself and the way others saw you. Somewhere in between was the 'truth' if such a thing really existed. But even the truth has a way of backfiring. At the end of her successful date with Candidate 125, Nina leaned in for the obligatory kiss and her date took a step back. He adjusted his glasses and cleared his throat.

"What's wrong?" asked Nina gently, thinking he was overcome with shyness.

"Look, I don't want to hurt your feelings," he said. "But you're really not my type. You're a nice girl and everything and very pretty but you're nowhere near as adventurous as you were online."

The day after Nina posted her most recent blog, Fallon called.

"Your stats are dropping. Your viewer count is low mitigated in part by your last date, which was a total disaster. How will anyone believe they can find love online when someone with your looks gets dumped by, what did he call himself? An *adrenaline* junkie? You're going to have to come up with something to make the blog more enticing."

"I'm going on the dates. I'm writing a book. Isn't that enough?"

"No. It isn't enough to write about your experiences. You have to put in more time and effort, the way other bloggers do. You have to be worthy of your followers. You have to be seriously committed," said Fallon.

"Going out with a different man every day for every day of the year isn't commitment enough?"

"Not when others are raising the bar. There is a man in Michigan who has decided not to speak anymore. He's documenting it all, of course. There's a couple in France pledging to have sex with one other every single day, God help them. Your audience wants romance served on a silver platter. What you're serving is disillusion. I'm putting you in touch with our head of marketing. He has some clever ideas."

Ronald, rehashed all the interesting things he had seen online: weddings dances, childbirth videos, owners posting photos of fucking cats who looked like fucking Hitler.

"How about something like that?"

"You want me to give birth online?" asked Nina.

"Not exactly," said Ronald, chortling. "But something catchy and gimmicky and heart-warming. Just think of something because your losing readers."

That evening Nina went to her storeroom where she kept her files. Hundreds of love notes, boxes of handwritten letters, postcards and mementos, chat logs on floppy disks and memory sticks, character sheets, checklists, before and after impressions written on napkins, thousands of words written about online relationships on printer paper, construction pads and composition notebooks. There were plain journals, seashell journals, journals with clouds and flowers and cats, on recycled card, fabric and leather, all categorized neatly by date, candidate, and subject matter. Nina carried out her life's work, dragging it piece-by-piece into the living room. Boxes and notebooks spilled out everywhere. There were sheets scattered on tables, couches, and chairs. Notes on window ledges and inside the unlit fireplace. Index cards were spread over every surface, lost under bookcases and stuck between the sofa pillows and floorboards of her apartment.

Do people have any idea how hard I've worked on my book? Nina thought, sitting on a stack of papers. "Hyenas," she muttered under her breath. She took another gulp of wine. Worse than hyenas. Animals didn't wait for you to fall on your sword so they could laugh about your blog with their friends. Even though she was putting herself out there every night, her readers were bored. Once the novelty had worn off they were onto the next new thing. They didn't want to read about reinvention or how hard it was to find a person they were compatible with. They didn't want to hear how it took time and effort to really get to know someone. They wanted Nina to tell them how easy it was to fall in love.

The Internet was a circus act, complete with ringmaster, dancing ponies and flames and Nina had stupidly added herself to the line-up as a clown or some annoying juggler.

All she wanted was to get people's attention. Her blog was never supposed to be the main attraction. What Nina really wanted was the chance to explain how to improve a person's chances in love. She wanted to detail how to assess an online paramour's tastes in music and films by asking a series of specific questions, rather than taking their word for it. She had entire sections on how to spot a pretender and how to read between the lines. Pauses, Nina wrote, were as strong an indicator as replies, if you knew what to look for. But now the book was going to be buried and no one would benefit from her knowledge. Who wanted to get romantic advice from a serial dater who couldn't even bag a blind date?

Nina picked up a journal circa 1995 from the floor and smoothed out the pages. She missed the rush of those early days, the tender details of her first online encounters preserved in her notebooks like pressed flower petals.

She had written about her meet-ups, copying entire conversations, snippets of emails, even dialogues from phone conversations. The entries still sounded exciting, surprising even, the initial delight of meeting people halfway around the world and not knowing what to expect. All that potential, all those ideas, and several years later the Internet had grown into a spoiled child, part erroneous encyclopaedia, part global shopping mall, part bulletin board where you posted comments and fake sepia photos for the approval of others.

How were you supposed to navigate your way around enough to find a compatible person you were interested in? Nina had started writing her how-to-guide, long before the web was teeming with self-aware Facebook fans, with tweeters and bloggers and instagrammers all vying for attention. Nowadays, even school kids knew how to sell themselves.

Fallon was right about one thing: Nina could not continue writing about her loser dates, waiting for her readers to lose interest. At this rate her publishers would drop her and her book.

Nina sat there until the sun came up, literally weighed down by her past. The sum of all those wonderful meets, romantic conversations and interesting characters in her notebooks were easily 100 times more exciting than any date she'd been on recently. But why? Was it all to do with lack of expectation or were there truly no more surprises left? And just like that Nina knew what she had to do. If her readers wanted romance, she would give it to them. She would serve it up to them on a platter and do what any entrepreneurial and sophisticated person of revolutionary ideas and letters did when they were stuck. She would make the shit up.

THE RULES

To: Nina Parks
Re: 365 Dates Blog
From: Iguana Blue Publishing
Dear Ms Parks,

After speaking to your Editor about project '365 Dates', we have drafted a set of guidelines we would like you to adhere to. We ask that you review and sign the attached document and forward a copy to our legal department as soon as possible.

Signed,
The Publishing team

    1. Contact with candidates and subsequent interchanges must be established online through textual communication (i.e. chat, Facebook, Twitter)

    2. At no time should there be pre-date exchange of phone calls, photos or videos.

3. NP is not allowed to cancel dates. If she does not show up by the required time, the date will be null and void and not count toward the 365 dates.

4. Candidates will be referred to by number, not name. NP may not use her own real name or discuss the book or blog at any time, with any person.

5. No outside dating, i.e. 'personal interests' during the 365 days of the project.

6. NP must respond to any questions and comments from blog readers.

7. All material collected from the project, falls under the copyright of contractual agreement and remains the intellectual property of the publisher.

TWENTY SONGS OF LOVE

MrSmith: Hello? Is anyone out there? Hello? Anyone?

Chicklit: Hey.

MrSmith: Hurray. We have contact. Excellent. ASL?

Chicklit: You've got to be kidding. Age/Sex/Location? How very retro. Age is irrelevant, location is ridiculous (considering where we are) and sex is out of the question if you go around ASLing people.

MrSmith: I thought ASL was a standard greeting among your kind. Like Live Long and Prosper.

Chicklit: You've been sadly misinformed by the Dummy's Guide to Chatting up Girls on the Internet.

MrSmith: There's a guide for that?

Chicklit: Look, ASL is the chat equivalent of *baby what's your star sign*. That tag will never bag you anyone interesting. Most of us aren't here to be picked off trees like cherries.

MrSmith: Cherries grow on trees? I always thought they grew in the ground. See, that's what city living does to a man.

Chicklit rolls her eyes.

MrSmith: Cool! Third person action. How did you do that?

Chicklit: Read your manual.

MrSmith: Okay. Point taken, Miss or is it Mrs. Chicklit?

Chicklit: Unbelievable.

MrSmith: Did I get it wrong again? I'm not very good at this.

Chicklit: Really? I couldn't tell.

MrSmith: Sarcasm. Great. Something I do understand. You must be warming to me. So are you or aren't you?

Chicklit: ?

MrSmith: Single, free, available? I assume the Chick in your name refers to a woman but you could be a robot. It's hard to tell from this angle.

Chicklit: Wow, you really are lousy at this. *Here* it doesn't matter what my status is. For all you know, I am a guy pretending to be a woman, pretending to be a robot in drag. And NONE of us are interested in you. I'm here to chat. Not to flirt with strange men who don't know that cherries grow on trees.

MrSmith: You think I'm strange? My heart just skipped a beat. But when you say *here* you mean in space, right?

Chicklit: LOL. I'm NOT in space. Though it might explain your behaviour.

MrSmith: So what do you call this?

Chicklit: Call what?

MrSmith: THIS. This thing we are standing in, talking in, typing to one another in. This receptacle that holds our thoughts and silly third person actions.

Chicklit sighs.

MrSmith: I know I'm not articulating it properly, but we're connecting in a way I've never experienced, aren't we? It's a little overwhelming.

Chicklit: Newbie.

MrSmith: I did say this was my first time. Please be gentle.

Chicklit: So now you want me to hold your hand?

MrSmith: Fine. I'm going to pretend you've welcomed me and this is your version of *mi casa es tu casa*. So what do you do when you are not instructing Neanderthals on the finer protocols of chat?

Chicklit: Write.

MrSmith: Really? What do you write?

Chicklit: Poetry, mainly.

MrSmith: You make a living from that? I'm impressed.

Chicklit: Don't be. I'm actually a teacher.

MrSmith: Oh wow. I'm impressed. You teach like actual kids?

Chicklit: Oh yeah, when they're young they're great, so receptive and imaginative. That is, until they grow self-conscious. Then we stick them in cages and poke them with sticks.

MrSmith: So nothing's changed since I was little.

Chicklit: I'm afraid to ask what you do for a living. I hope it isn't agricultural.

MrSmith: Nowhere near that interesting. I'm a lawyer.

Chicklit: A lawyer who reads Neruda?

MrSmith: Hum?

Chicklit: A lawyer who has a sense of humour.

MrSmith: I'm flattered, but I'm afraid I don't know who/what this Neruda of yours is.

Chicklit: You've never heard of Pablo Neruda?

MrSmith: No. But you're making me feel like I should.

Chicklit: He's a famous poet. Won the Nobel Prize?

MrSmith: What year?

Chicklit: Year? Why is that relevant?

MrSmith: It isn't. I'm just curious.

Chicklit: He's one of the greatest love poets of the twentieth century. How could you not have heard of him?

MrSmith: I don't have time to read poetry. Too busy saving the world.

Chicklit: I can't believe you said that.

MrSmith: For a robot in drag you are strangely lacking in humour.

Chicklit: How about *Twenty Love Poems and a Song of Despair?*

MrSmith: Yes, please, but I could do without the despair.

Chicklit: Doesn't it ring a bell?

MrSmith: Nope. Should it?

Chicklit: You are *IN* it.

MrSmith: How does one do a third person action for completely baffled?

Chicklit: Smith, this chatroom is named after Neruda's famous book of poems.

MrSmith: Oh! No wonder it sounded familiar.

Chicklit: Did you read the instructions before joining this chatroom?

MrSmith: No I didn't get that memo.

Chicklit: *For fans of Neruda and his writing. No trolls, hackers, or lurkers.*

MrSmith: I can't say if I am a troll or a lurker, because I honestly have no idea what those are.

Chicklit: A *troll* is someone who joins only to cause trouble. A *lurker* is someone who never participates in a chat, just sits in the shadows and lurks. Which are you?

MrSmith: Neither. It just sounded like an interesting name for a chatroom.

Chicklit: You are kidding, right?

MrSmith: No. My discovery of your tree house was a happy coincidence. I've never read 20 songs of love and I'm not a big fan of poetry. I'm afraid my young mind was never very receptive.

Chicklit counts slowly to ten.

MrSmith: Are you getting the pointy stick?

Chicklit: No need. It's a lost cause.

MrSmith: Wait, I'm willing to learn. Go on, share you nuggets of wisdom. I'm a firm believer in 'never too late'. That is of course unless it really *is* too late, in which case it doesn't look good for me.

Chicklit: It *never* looked good for you.

MrSmith: Ouch. You're a tough cookie.

Chicklit: You can't even get the title of Neruda's book right. It isn't 20 Songs of Love, it's Twenty Love *Poems*.

MrSmith: You always such a stickler for detail? How do your students survive?

Chicklit: Most of them pay attention. Can't say the same for you.

MrSmith: I'm going to ignore that because:

a. I do pay attention

b. What makes this Neruda guy so special? Presumably they don't just hand out Nobels?

c. You seem a tad pedantic about names of things. I'll try not to construe what that means about you as a person.

Chicklit: I'm not getting pulled into this argument.

MrSmith: Because I'm right?

Chicklit: Neruda's poetry encapsulates the feeling of being head over heels in love, of tasting and seeing things with passionate eyes. This from a man who understood the world and politics. A man who was exiled from his own home. It didn't turn him into a cynic. He continued trying to capture the beauty of humanity. Are YOU able to do that?

MrSmith: Love? That's why he got a Nobel? He didn't postulate a theory? Discover anything new?

Chicklit: So scientists are the only ones who deserve prizes? Please tell me what's so special about inventing weapons or technology that will hurt others?

MrSmith: I'm not being a jerk here, but with so many people who need food and medical care, your answer is poetry? Come on.

Chicklit: I can't believe you're so narrow-minded. Poetry has helped those in despair, the subjugated, those without hope or light. But to understand it, you have to have a sliver of a soul.

MrSmith: I'm not discrediting all poets, but how can you believe that words make up the meat and potatoes of love? They don't compare to the way the back of a lover's neck smells, or the way their legs intertwine with yours so that you don't even know whose legs they are.

Chicklit: Exactly. That's what I mean. You can evoke emotion by using the right words. You just did it right now.

MrSmith: I think a lot of your writing heroes wouldn't have bothered if they had someone who returned their affections. If Keats or Poe or any of those guys had someone who reciprocated their feelings, they would have been too busy getting it on to mope.

Chicklit: That's not really the point.

MrSmith: Yeah? How can you write about love if you've never experienced it? Words are a poor substitute. That's all I'm saying.

Chicklit: Have you ever felt passion so intense it made you forget everything? Made you believe you existed only for that specific person?

MrSmith: No. But you are making me wish I had.

Chicklit: That's what poetry does. It captures that moment.

MrSmith: But why call it poetry? Call it pretty words to help you get laid.

Chicklit: I give up.

MrSmith: Hey, you're the one that implied I have no soul.

Chicklit:

MrSmith: Hello?

Chicklit:

MrSmith: Chicklit, are you there?

Chicklit:

MrSmith: I was just kidding. Come back and we'll talk more about Neruda and love or whatever.

Chicklit:

MrSmith: I guess you don't want to talk anymore?

Chicklit:

MrSmith: Fine. I'll just sit here and talk to myself.

Chicklit:

MrSmith: So, it's your way or no way at all? That's pretty dictatorial for someone who is into communist poets.

Chicklit:

MrSmith: How do I know he's a communist? I Googled him while I was waiting for you to come back. I like his Ode to Salt. You have to admire a man who can create works of art at the breakfast table.

Chicklit:

MrSmith: Are you really not going to respond? Fine. Your loss. This could have been the start of a wonderful friendship. But now we'll never know. You talk a good game. All for love and love for all, but when it comes down to it, you're just as scared as everyone else.

Chicklit:

MrSmith: I'm going now.

<MrSmith logs off at 23:05>

Chicklit:

Chicklit:

<Chicklit logs off at 23:10>

KEEPER OF MEMORY

HE POPS INTO my life out of nowhere, saying he wants to meet.

"Come on, Jillian, it will be fun," he messages. "We'll rehash the past over a beer or two. Fifteen years deserves as much. Don't you think?"

He found me on Facebook a few weeks ago. I was hoping his photo would trigger some memory of his name or face, but there was a blank where his face should be. A blank superimposed by a question mark.

Now I know what you're thinking. If I didn't remember him, why did I accept his Facebook friendship? But it's no big deal. I know hundreds of people I've never met. We run in the same circles, have the same interests, which is reason enough to connect, I suppose. Virtual strangers understand space. They stay at a distance I'm comfortable with. Not like the people I actually know: old boyfriends, relatives, former classmates—always reminiscing and filling my wall up with the past.

"There is nothing glorious about nostalgia," I want to say, but there's no avoiding them. They come at me incessantly like zombies. Except, instead of brains they want memories. I add them as friends and ignore them, wondering how people stayed in touch with people they didn't want to stay in touch with before the days of social networking.

"I genuinely want to see you. What do you say? Have a drink with an old *new* friend?"

I tell him that having been friends fifteen years ago is not the same as a fifteen-year friendship. Also, I'm busy.

"Oh, I get it. You're scared."

"Don't be silly. What would I be scared of?"

"Memories. Of ghosts from your past. You are scared of reconnecting."

"No. I told you, I have something to do that weekend. Ask me again when we hit our twenty-fifth year of not being friends."

He's disappointed. I can tell. He thought I'd jump at the chance to reunite. The old me would have, but that was long ago, back when I was fearless. My new look is reserved, careful. I tell people it's my maturity costume. Except the transformation is happening under the surface. If you look closely, you can see it rippling and flexing beneath my skin like muscle.

"Do you even remember who I am?"

"Of course," I lie.

In case you are wondering, I don't usually forget people. Well, not in the way others forget: confusedly, haltingly, piecemeal, as if they were recollecting dreams. My absence of memory, when it happens, is brutal and absolute. A backdrop of shocking white.

That evening I sit with my microwave dinner and sift through my old emails. After an hour of searching, I give up. I don't know what I thought I'd find. My emails only go back a year. Most of them get deleted as soon as I read them.

It wasn't always that way. When I was younger, I saved everything: photos, letters, diaries. I even saved the menus from romantic dinners.

Deleting was a gradual process. Moving from house to house, from partner to partner, I started losing parts of myself. No one ever tells you that. No one tells you that you have a finite amount of yourself to give before the bottom goes out, before you close down, turn away from new experiences, become an emotional recluse. When that happens, the love letters and keepsakes are constant reminders of your failure to stay connected.

Better to be uncluttered. *Sans* baggage. Your past is irreconcilable anyway. The more you try to hold on, the faster it turns to sand in your hands. Take it from me, the world is divided into two kinds of people: those who willingly forget, and those who drag their pasts around in boxes forever talking about how things used to be.

The following morning I contact Nina Parks. I know Nina from my university days, before she became a self-help author and expert on how to find love on the Internet. Nina remembers everyone.

"Sorry his name doesn't ring a bell. Are you sure he knows you? Maybe he's confusing you with someone else? Maybe he's pretending to know you?"

"I don't think so. He remembers specific details. He described my dorm room, down to the titles of the books on my shelf."

"Let me get this straight. This possible boyfriend came to see you years ago, you don't remember anything about him, but you still remember your books?"

"It's not that strange. People are transient. I met a lot of people in those days."

"So did I, but I never blanked anyone. Look, I'm worried about you. This isn't the first time you've forgotten something major."

"This isn't major. I'm just curious. Do you still keep everything? All your emails and letters chronologically and meticulously backed up?"

"Of course. How else do you think I remember?"

"Can you please check your archives? I may have written something to you that will spark a memory."

"I'll check, but don't hold your breath. Chances are if you don't remember him, then he must not have left much of an impression. Some people are best forgotten."

"But you don't forget anyone, do you?"

"No."

"Even boring people?"

"I make it a point to specifically remember those."

After I hang up the phone, I brush my teeth and go to bed. For the past few days I've been unable to sleep, too worried I might be losing my mind. I've wilfully ejected so many negative events, that my brain seems to be automatically self-assessing my memories, deciding what stays and what goes.

The same thing happened to my mother, who had a traumatic childhood she never liked to talk about. She forced herself to block out everything in an effort to get over her past. "People put too much stock in remembering. Forgetfulness is bliss," she used to say.

But it backfired. My mother always forgot the little things as well as the major events of her life: appointments, something left in the oven, the names of her children. When the neighbours called to say she'd locked herself out of her house again, I knew it was serious. I found mom sitting on the steps of her house, staring blankly at the world around her.

"I don't know how I got here," she would say, frightened. "How can I have forgotten an entire morning?"

At the nursing home things weren't much better. My mother could describe events with extraordinary detail: a china doll she had as a child, the blue dress she wore to the registry office when she married my father, her pet iguana named Ernesto, but her recall was random---a sure sign she was deteriorating. Births, weddings and deaths disappeared from her memory banks as if someone had hit the delete key. She would freeze in mid-sentence and you could see the bridges burning, leaving her stranded on little islands of memory. Within a year my mother's mind was wiped clean. At age 66, she was unable to recognize anyone. Not me. Not my sisters. Not even herself.

That night in my dreams, an image of a tall man floats to the surface, rustling like a solitary leaf in autumn. I latch on to it, unable to tell if the memory is real or if it's Memorex. It feels superimposed. The way I would sometimes take a photo of a boy in school I had a crush on and paste him into one of my pictures.

Mystery Man instant messages me the next day.

MM: So what do I have to do to convince you to have a drink with me?

Jillian: Stop trying to convince me for starters.

MM: Don't overthink it. Just say what comes to mind.

Jillian: Fine. The answer is no.

MM: Why not?

Jillian: Because the past is the past. It's not 1995 anymore. We've grown up and moved on.

MM: Was I so awful back then?

Jillian: We were all pretty awful. We were young and stupid college kids.

MM: You don't remember me, do you? Not one little bit.

"Of course I do," I type, feeling a tinge of sadness for my lost memory. I may not have recalled him specifically or the nature of our relationship, but we'd had discourse. Our paths crossed. We'd been friends. That was significant in the scheme of things and I wanted to acknowledge that connection. Except I'm a different person now.

Nina calls me later that evening. "Do you want the good news or the bad?"

"Bad first," I say, preparing myself for the worst.

"First, tell me what's going on. Who is this guy?"

"No one. That's the truth. He came out of nowhere. I just wanted to make sure he wasn't making things up."

"I couldn't find any evidence of him," Nina says. "Maybe he is who he says he was, but I don't remember you talking about him, which is very unlike you. You used to talk incessantly about men you were infatuated with."

"Yes, but you were busy that summer."

"Was I?"

"Yep, brooding over that guy with the goatee who thought he was the next Thom Yorke."

"There you go. That's the good news."

"Nina, stop being cryptic."

"The good news is you're not losing your memory, Jones. You remembered something even I had forgotten. I did foolishly chase whatshisname. God, that was a long time ago."

"So what you're saying is there isn't any good news?"

Nina may have been a renowned expert on Internet dating but she could be frustratingly self-absorbed, not to mention smug. I wonder if she remembered that it was me who introduced her to chat.

"Here's a suggestion. Why don't you give Mystery Man a chance? So what if you don't remember? It might be fun to go for drinks anyway. Play it by ear and see what happens. Don't be so afraid of everything. You're a risk-taker, for God's sake. You used to jump out of planes."

Nina doesn't get it. She never has. She has no problems with men or heartbreak. Back at university she was the *femme fatale* of the online world, flirting and wooing her way through life, while I was always waiting for the perfect man. Perhaps I did find him but was too involved to realize it. Worse than that, maybe I found him, let him go, and erased the entire thing from my mind.

I don't bother to finish my dinner, going to bed miserable for the third night in a row.

I try to recall when I became so safe. I used to be the first to launch myself in the water, no matter how cold or deep. I was the one who told everyone else that it was OK to go in. Somehow, I became prudent, the cautious one, the swimmer afraid of the undertow. Now I won't even go in. I stand by the edge of the water watching everyone else have fun.

"So tell me," I say to him. "Do you genuinely remember me or is this all a ruse?"

MM: You know what it was like back then. Online you could meet a new person every five seconds. I must have fallen in love twenty times that year.

Jillian: But not with me.

MM: Not really.

Jillian: Great. Now I'm sorry I asked.

MM: Don't be. You were the one who wanted to keep it platonic.

Jillian: Do you blame me? What with you falling in love every five seconds.

MM: Falling in love means nothing if you don't recall the person years later. I remember you. Vividly.

I know he's not being truthful, but my heart, silly, optimistic little organ, doesn't know the difference between hope and reality. I want Mystery Man to remember me with a desperation that startles me. Then again, who doesn't want to be remembered through the years like some unforgettable lover? *Unforgettable.* Even the word is romantic.

Jillian: Give me a break.

MM: Sorry. I had to try. I was hoping you'd bite. Everyone else has.

Jillian: Everyone?

MM: Fourteen at last count. You weren't the only one. Of the twenty-three women I contacted, fourteen responded. There would have been more, but I couldn't locate them all.

Jillian: Let me get this straight. You claim to have powers of the past, and women, dozens of them, agree to go out with you?

MM: It's official. I'm more popular now than I was in my 20s. I'm planning a road trip to meet them. I'd like to see you too.

Jillian: Oh, I'm definitely not having drinks with you now.

MM: Why not?

Jillian: Because you're lying to all those women. To me. You're exploiting our forgetfulness.

MM: I'm not exploiting, I'm exploring new opportunities.

Jillian: But we aren't *new*. You're trying to recapture your past, yet everything you did back then belongs to a different person. Isn't it time to stop dredging Lake Memory?

MM: I can't pretend my past is composed of empty space. You meant something to me, Jillian. You all did. I don't dismiss connections because I can't recall every detail. Fifteen years is fifteen years.

Jillian: Fifteen years is a pimple on the face of time.

MM: I don't understand how you can be so blasé.

Jillian: Look, we were an intersection. A blip on the road to nowhere. I don't need to revisit every inconsequential relationship. *You* are the one hocking memories.

MM: It's not like that.

Jillian: Really? Because I'm going to be straight with you, I don't remember anything about you. Not one single thing. Don't take it personally. I'm just good at deleting people from my life. I don't mean to. It just happens.

MM: You don't save old emails?

Jillian: Why should I be attached to dead things that can't breathe or grow, they only serve to remind you what you can never get back.

The parlance for rejecting someone never changes. Be kind but firm. That's the best way to do it. Sorry, I don't want to see you. Sorry, I've moved on. Sorry, it's best we don't speak to one another anymore.

He is silent for the first time since our re-acquaintance. I wonder again at this strange connection of ours, where neither of us recall the details of our friendship, if indeed we were ever friends.

Someone should warn you that one day your recall will go. That way, when you are younger you can commit everything to memory. Forget forgetting. Cram all those moments down like an overfed goose. Make crib notes on your arms and legs, slip in pieces of paper into the very recess of forgetfulness so that you'll be prepared. Given the chance, I would have kept everything, because time has a way of condescending all those years into a blur. Only factual stuff is left, and even that amounts to no more than a few footnotes. The date of my birth. The day my mother died. Christmas 1994. Emotions have long been stripped from my memories. I was conscious that I'd done all the forgetting on purpose, to save myself pain. It had left me incomplete, Holey—a blank slate where there should be something.

MM: Has anyone told you that you have an unhealthy perspective of the past?

Jillian: Says the man going around pretending he remembers people just to get laid.

MM: That's not fair. I've done a lot of soul searching to get here. If it helps, I am no longer the smug, insensitive, self-righteous bastard I'm certain I once was.

Jillian: Smug? Self righteous? Wait, I do remember you.

MM: Very funny. Look, this is my chance to find the parts of myself I've scattered around. People are looking forward to seeing me. I'm not just taking up their time. I'm giving something in return. What you can't remember, you reinvent.

Jillian: You should get that printed on a t-shirt.

MM: You know what every woman wants to hear? That they haven't changed. That they haven't grown old and disillusioned. That they are still as capable of love as they were all those years ago.

Jillian: Yeah, but we have changed. There's no way around it. How do you make peace with the past? You know, your true memories.

MM: There's no such thing.

Jillian: What do you mean? Events happened. Facts don't change.

MM: You talk about the past, but you don't really understand. Nothing is set in stone. What you choose to remember is as truthful as the things you forget.

Jillian: That's called lying.

MM: No, it is called living with imperfect memories. Your version of the past is not the same as mine.

Jillian: You've got that right. Unlike you, I don't want some re-imagining of what I was like. I want the truth or nothing. I'll tell you what, if you can come up with one genuine memory, I'll have drinks with you. And no looking at your old emails. From memory.

MM: Piece of cake. Let's see. You had long brown hair, a thing for cherry lip-gloss. You wore hippie chick dresses and long boots.

Jillian: You sound like Hannibal Lecter. Besides, that could be any girl from the 90s. You're going to have to do better than that.

I don't want him to show me snapshots of the past. Having someone describe what you were like is as bad as looking at unflattering photographs. What I really want to know is if he remembers me as more than lips and hair. I want him to describe my laughter, the way I looked when things didn't go my way. *Fearless.* I want him to tell me I was fearless.

MM: What do you want? I gave you details.

Jillian: See? I knew you didn't have anything concrete. I'm going. Don't contact me again.

MM: Wait. The first time we met, we went to an old bar near your apartment, an awful place full of lounge lizards. Sky something or other. The bartender wouldn't serve us, so we went back to your place.

Jillian: Go on.

MM: You had a bottle of vodka and we climbed to the roof. I told you I was scared of heights, so you sang Radiohead songs to distract me. One of your neighbours threatened to call the cops. You sang louder. Afterward, you held my hand and pointed out the stars. That night has stayed with me all these years.

Despite my reservations, I swallow every word. My past self, invented or not, sounds wonderfully gutsy. Fiction or reality, it doesn't matter. The version he's telling me is the one I want most to believe.

FROM THE ART OF
GIVING GOOD CHAT

From The Ultimate Guide to Finding Love Online by Nina Parks

1. Developing good rapport takes time. Build it up slowly while getting to know each other. Ask questions. Amaze them with your wit and intelligence. Don't rush into meeting right away.

2. Don't monopolize the dialogue. Discuss things you are both interested in. Good conversation is about listening as much as it is about knowing what to say.

3. Repeatedly talking about the same topics is as exciting as comparing shopping lists. Force yourself to come out of your comfort zone. You don't want to eat porridge every day, do you? Spice it up by bringing up new and interesting ideas.

4. Learn to listen. I can't stress how important this is. I'll write more later on the subject of online flirtation, but for now, let me say that the most appealing thing you can do is pay attention to what the other person is saying.

5. Be confident. No matter if you are pretending to be someone else, you can still be yourself at the core.

6. Learn to laugh. At yourself mainly, but at other things that can't always be controlled. I'm not suggesting you act flighty or air-headed, but being too serious, without the ability to be self-deprecating, is a serious hindrance.

7. Finally, know when to move on. If romance or friendship isn't in the cards, find someone else. Plenty of other chatters will be interested in what you have to say. Don't waste your time by forcing a connection.

COMIC BOOKS AND FRENCH KISSES

FLORENCE ATE A crust-less peanut butter sandwich and steamed open the envelope containing her report card. As expected, it featured mostly red-inked marks and an attached page of comments from her teacher, informing her mother that Florence wasn't living up to her full potential.

Florence brushed whiteout on her grades, transforming Ds into Cs. She sat back to admire her handiwork, then placed the letter back in the envelope and resealed it with glue. Her report cards were always the same. If students had a section for rebuttals, Florence would write: another boring, tedious year of teachers who don't inspire me to live up to my 'potential'--whatever that means. She retrieved the rest of the day's mail and organized it into little piles on the coffee table.

Pile one consisted of her mother's bills and letters.

Pile two was for supermarket coupons and magazines.

Pile three (the largest) was everything addressed to her.

You would think a twelve-year old girl wouldn't get much mail, but by age seven, Florence was sending off for decoder rings and x-ray glasses without any help. She progressed to product samples, recipes and mailing labels advertised in the back of her mother's magazines. She kept her cut-outs arranged alphabetically in color-coded ring binders she stored under her bed. Every night before she went to sleep, she tallied her booty in an old ledger, keeping track of exactly how many labels from cans of soup and cereals she needed for free merchandise. When she grew bored of that game, Florence invented new personas and sent off for things in their names as well.

"Why have they delivered Mr. Flushbumm's *Senior Prevention* here again?" Her mother, Frankie asked. "Last week it was Emily Einstein's *Cosmo*. I'm going to call the post office and set them straight."

"Ma, please don't. They're for me. I sent off for them."

"Are you telling me you are Emily Einstein?"

"Sort of. Yes."

Frankie drew in a sharp breath.

"I'm sorry ma, I thought you could use some free magazines."

"First of all, it's wrong to willingly deceive the post office. It's probably also illegal. Frankie put her feet up on the coffee table and closed her eyes. "I know you're trying to help, but if you focused on your schoolwork with the same intensity as you do with your *extracurricular* activities, you wouldn't be flunking English."

"But look at all the money I've saved."

'It's my job to worry about money. Yours is to do well in school. Don't you want to go to college? Or do you want to end up like me, cleaning offices?"

Florence, who occasionally helped Frankie on weekends, hated cleaning only slightly less than she hated school, but she never argued with her mother.

"I've spoken to your teachers," her mother continued without opening her eyes. We've agreed that you will spend your after school hours in a remedial reading program."

"But..."

"I don't want to hear another word." Frankie sat up and levelled a 'don't even think of disobeying me' look at her daughter. "Your test scores are pitiful. Your report cards lousy. You might even be kept a year behind, despite what your new report card says."

Florence hung her head.

"A smart, resourceful girl getting such bad grades." Frankie shook her head. "I explained to your teachers that all you do at home is read and write, but they want you to do your work in class. So until your grades improve, the packages and magazines will stop. I'm putting your stamps and binders away, in case you have other ideas. And you will attend remedial studies."

Florence met with Miss Clark on Monday, Wednesday and Friday afternoons. Together, they would choose a book (primers, they called them) and she would read it aloud to her teacher. Most of the books were for a much younger age group and consisted of animals that talked or magical fruit. The text was so large it only contained a paragraph or two on each page. Afterward, Florence had to answer questions to test her comprehension. Miss Clark was always hovering nearby, making clucking sounds when Florence grew bored or distracted. "Are you sure that's the correct answer," she would say, when Florence mindlessly shaded in the multiple choice dots with her pencil.

The only good thing about Remedial happened at the end of class. If Florence had performed well, Miss Clark allowed her to choose from a pile of educational glossy booklets, foldout nutritional pyramids and charts depicting the human body. Sometimes there were larger-than-life-sized posters of athletes spouting motivational quotes.

'WITH HARD WORK YOU CAN ACHIEVE ANYTHING'
'ONLY A TRUE WINNER CAN OVERCOME ADVERSITY'
'BELIEVE...'

Florence papered her bedroom with these platitudes and fell asleep every night looking up at the exhausted but victorious faces of mountain climbers and champion figure skaters. Part of her hoped that while she was sleeping, a little bit of inspiration would rub off and she'd wake up knowing what she wanted to do with her life.

One day, Miss Clark showed up to class with envelopes. "Your mother tells me you love writing letters?" Florence sat up straight, for once paying attention as Miss Clark breathlessly talked of someone called Elizabeth Barrett, who fell in love with someone else called Robert Browning. Shy and painfully withdrawn, every day was torture for poor little Elizabeth, Miss Clark said, clicking her tongue. "Imagine what it must have been like to wait every day by the window, pining for the postman."

Florence didn't know a thing about poetry or romance, but she did know how it felt to wait for the postman. There was nothing as exciting as the breathless anticipation that ate away at her belly, as she ran home from school, wondering if there was an envelope waiting. When there was, it was always a wonderful surprise, even if it was only a magazine. It made Florence feel special to know she, of all people, was worthy of receiving a package or envelope from a total stranger. Later on, those practiced skills in patience and pining would come in handy.

"Now pay attention, Florence, A good correspondent does more than just put down words on paper. You have to engage your reader. Keep them interested. Make them really look forward to replying to your letter." Miss Clark handed her an envelope. "We're going to write to Mr. Johnson from your science class. We're going to ask him what he thinks about your proposal for next year's science fair. What do you think of that?"

Miss Clark all but wrote that first letter. Florence just signed her name at the bottom.

"Well, I will say this for you, Florence. You have excellent penmanship. Now let's put it in his cubbyhole and see what he says."

No stamp? No visit to the post office? What was the point of pretending it was a real letter?

A week later, she asked Miss Clark for the twentieth time why Mr. Johnson still hadn't responded. "He must be busy, I'm sure. Let's give him another week."

But he never replied.

"This illustrates what I was saying," said her teacher. "It's important to write in an *engaging* manner to be taken seriously. Let's try writing to Mr. Reynolds, the custodian, instead."

Florence had a better idea. On her way home from school, she stopped at the library and found a list of names and addresses of people who appreciated being written to. People (unlike Mr. Johnson) who had the time and inclination to reply. When Frankie discovered her daughter had been writing to a young man in a correctional facility, she lost her mind. She dragged Florence to school and showed Miss Clark and the principal the letters they'd secretly been writing back and forth for months.

"Does this look like the work of a remedial reader?"

"You must promise to write to people your own age. Students," said Miss Clark. "If you want, you can correspond with international penpals. Let me get you started. *Bonjour, je voudrais un correspondant francais*," she wrote neatly and in large letters on top of a clean sheet of paper.

"But I don't speak French."

Miss Clark neatly crossed out the line. "Fine, we'll work on that. Why don't we stick to penpals that speak English?"

James 'Bigbee' McCullen was the first person to reply to one of Florence's letters. He was fourteen, a fan of football, *'soccer as you yanks call it'*, and he lived in Aberdeen, Scotland with his mother and stepfather. Even more than football, Bigbee was into comic books. He had been reading them since he was seven. He told her about his favourite shop where he and his friends hung out, his favourite superheroes and all the things she should read, if she wanted to start collecting comic books. He included a little drawing with his letter and sent it all in a large manila envelope.

Florence reciprocated immediately with a five-page reply doused in her mother's perfume. Unable to draw, she included cartoons cut out from an old *Readers Digest* and even sent him one of her smaller motivational posters, the one with the unicorn.

'BELIEVE…'

She didn't know if it was the distance or what, but it took Bigbee weeks to reply to her letter. When it finally arrived, it was written on a torn sheet of school paper.

Sorry I can't write you anymore. Have a girlfriend named Becca. I met her at school and she loves comics as much as I do! And she's a girl!! She can draw and everything too. She says her favourite things in the world are comic books and French kisses. No hard feelings. Bigbee.

PS: What gives with the Peanuts comic strip and the unicorn?

"Darling, don't waste your tears on him," Frankie said. "He lives halfway across the world. I want you to promise you'll forget those letters and spend more time on your studies."

Florence went to her room, took out her binder, scratched off Bigbee's name, selected a new sheet of paper and wrote to the next name on her list.

Jonas lived in Buenos Aires. The picture included with his letter, showed a brooding fifteen-year-old with sandy hair and eyebrows so thick, they looked like caterpillars had taken residence on his eyelids. He spoke English, as well as three other languages, loved books, and wanted to be a doctor just like his father.

Florence wrote back to say that she also loved books, real ones, not comics or primers. She was planning on teaching herself French over the summer. Maybe they could practice together? She told him her father was also a doctor, which was kind of true, as her dad was studying to get his doctorate in sociology. That was before he dropped out and ran away to live in Mexico with one of his fellow students, and from where he sent Florence the occasional postcard.

Unlike Bigbee, Jonas was a conscientious letter writer. Unfortunately, he was also sloppy, his lines penned with creative longhand, blotchy and difficult to decipher. He also had a habit of punctuating his sentences with expressive foreign words.

Interpreting Jonas's letters became Florence's new obsession. She sat at the table with several multilingual dictionaries, a magnifying glass and an out-of-date travel guide to Argentina that she found at the library.

Decoding his writing was only part of the game; the other consisted of responding to his ramshackle missives. Did he have three siblings or one? Was the family pet called Pedro or was that his brother's name? But no matter the effort, it was all worth it, because this time, Florence was sure her devotion was reciprocated. Jonas was smart and attentive and he liked her. That is until he set her straight. This time his words were crystal clear. The letter typed out on his father's old Corona.

Florence, I have <u>NO</u> idea why you are writing me all these CRAZY letters. Who the hell is Pedro? What a WEIRD Mädchen you are. How am I supposed to know who I will marry when I am older? MERDE! I am only 15!!!! I am not interested in a girlfriend. ALL I wanted was a PENPAL. If I wanted to find a girl, I would not choose you but someone who lives in BA. I'm too young for a SERIOUS relationship. Maybe later, when I'm older. COÑO! It isn't because you aren't pretty.

*You are molto bella. I even showed YOUR photograph to my
father who agrees, but PAPA says I need to concentrate on my
studies if I want to get into a good school. He said minas like
you are problématique and make MEN lose their heads. You
write so many letters yet none make sense. Capice? Despite
what you say, you don't seem VERY inteligente or you would
stop asking about my brothers. I said five times I am an hijo
unico. For clarification, I do not have a dog, cat, Byrd or any
animal. Horst! I am NOT YOUR inamorato! SO stop signing
all your letters, Always and Forever with hearts. I suggest you
get therpia _help_ soon, because you really need it! Please don't
write back. It is FINITO for us, pen pal. If you reply, I will say
Lutsch meine Eier. SI?*

This time the crying lasted for almost a month. Florence
locked herself in her bedroom and did not come out except to
go to school. She had put every ounce of energy and passion
into her letter writing — and for what? Everything she cared
about was doomed to failure.

Obsessive personality, her mother called it, but Florence
didn't know how else to be.

She carefully put her folders and mailing lists into a box,
wrapped it with packing tape, and stored it in the back of
her closet. At thirteen, she was much too old to sending out
for decoder rings.

She took Jonas' photograph and all his blotchy letters and
ripped them into shreds, which she mailed to him in Buenos
Aires, along with a note.

*Dear Jonas, I never expected you to think I liked you! Mon
dieu! I have a boyfriend. His name is Bigbee and we've been
going out for a year. He's much older than you but I prefer
older guys. Plus, he is an expert in French kissing, something
you don't know anything about, even though you say you are
fluent in French. You and I never had much in common. I
think doctors are very bourgeois. I'm sorry you misunderstood*

my intentions. I was only looking for someone to practice my Spanish with. In any case, please never write me again. If you do, I'll have to tell Bigbee and he gets very jealous, like the Incredible Hulk.

PS: My mother thinks you look like a German shepherd.

PSS: I looked up Lutsch meine Eier and you are DISGUSTING!

It took her a while, but when Florence finally got over Jonas, she was wiser, with that sad haunted look people sometimes get after grieving, her heart wrapped in four inches of protective tissue, but once and for all over her obsession with silly boys.

"I'm done with penpals," she told her mother. "From now on I am going to focus my energy on school."

"I'm glad," said Frankie. "Because it would be a tragedy if a girl as smart as you neglected her education. I had big plans when I was younger and look what happened? I met your father. I fell in love and gave him everything and he left us high and dry. Florence, if you let it, love will drag you into the sea like an undertow. It will spin you around until there is nothing left but sand in your pants and those little pebbles that cut your feet. Promise me you will be strong and not let some boy derail your hopes and dreams."

There it was — the endless story of love gone wrong. Her mother's heaviest artillery, aimed straight for Florence's heart.

"Don't worry ma, nothing is going to distract me. I'm going to breathe, eat, and sleep school. I'm going to be the most outstanding student ever. The best."

Frankie let out a sigh. "You know what we should do? Go out and splurge on milkshakes and fries. Anything you want."

"Maybe later, ma. I'm going to go to my room and start studying. Right this minute. I've wasted too much time already."

It was important to make her mother understand. She was never going to be like her, working a thankless job and raising a child by herself with no money. If her experience with Bigbee and Jonas had taught Florence anything, it was that boys were not worth the trouble. Not if you ended up alone, pining for a person who didn't care about you.

Frankie looked at her daughter as she leapt off the couch and sauntered away. She was getting taller and more and more beautiful every day. The neighbourhood gossips kept coming around, handing out unwanted advice on how to keep Florence from going 'bad', as if her daughter was an overripe banana instead of a teenager. "She'll turn into a wild child," they warned Frankie. "That restless type needs to be looked after, otherwise she is going to grow up to be trouble. Just like her father."

Florence, daydreaming at her desk, knew that boys weren't going to disappear from her life anytime soon. But her mother was right. She would have to learn to control her emotions or they would sweep her away like the sea. She vowed to be the type of person that moved on, who never clung to anything. In fact, Florence was never going to stand still if she could help it. She would flit like a queen bee from experience to experience, gaining knowledge but never outstaying her welcome. Never again having to deal with rejection or heartbreak of having her affections go unreciprocated.

And so in a way, the gossips won out in the end with their self-fulfilling prophecies. Florence went on to become the trouble they all warned about—a hip-swinging, Catholic school skirt wearing, husband-head-turning threat—the hottest thing Little Italy had seen this side of a Chicago pizza. As for love, well, that was another matter. As Florence AKA Nina Parks liked to say, love was highly overrated.

THE ART OF SNAIL MAIL

From The Ultimate Guide to Finding Love Online by Nina Parks

YOU WOULD THINK that a person who is all about instant gratification would not be blogging in defence of snail mail, but I'm a huge fan. I love letters. I love everything about them: the smell of the ink, the envelope, even the choice of stamp.

Come on, admit it, don't you get excited when you receive something in the post that isn't a bill or a flyer?

Say all you want about email being faster and more efficient, there are positive aspects to delayed gratification. For starters, it can be tantalisingly, teasingly, excruciatingly delicious to open a letter/package from a special someone who is trying to connect with you in more ways than virtually.

Remember this. In a textual romance, the most memorable cyber lovers are those who understand the importance of tangibility. Among my treasures: airline tickets to Fiji, a rare edition of Lady Chatterley, a 10-inch dildo with realistic malleable balls from a man who said it was taken from his own plaster cast. I've also received poems, drawings, theatre tickets, an orange tree, and a hilarious video of someone dancing to 'Get Down On It'.

Now it is your turn.

Pick up your lover's letter and measure the weight of it in your hands. See how deliberate it is? It didn't pop up randomly in your box. Care and planning were involved. Is the envelope scented? If so, count yourself lucky. Now look at the handwriting. *Really* look at it. Hold it up to the light. Analyse the way the writing slants. Take your time. Remember that *they* have touched the envelope. Your paramour's tongue has licked the flap and the stamp. Perhaps he has lovingly held the letter close to his chest and kissed it for luck before sending. When you are ready, open it slowly. With a letter opener if you have one. Mine is silver with a mother of pearl handle. But if restraint gives way to desperation, by all means use your fingernails, teeth, whatever is at hand.

Some of you have written to ask if I recommend typing your letter in Word and then printing it out rather than writing it by hand. I cannot express how much I dislike this suggestion! A typed letter is ONLY appropriate in a professional capacity. You wouldn't expect a business letter to be handwritten, just as you would not type out your Christmas cards or wedding invitations.

Besides, a typed letter without the benefit of blotches and grammatical quirks will not give you an accurate impression of your lover. A good letter should contain imperfections in order to better highlight individuality. If it doesn't, ask yourself what your paramour is hiding. That brings me to my next topic. SAFETY.

1. Give your address out only to people you trust.

2. If you're unsure, have your mail delivered to a P.O. box.

3. Always examine the handwriting!

While letter writing can be great fun, don't forget the importance of penmanship, as it can reveal a number of interesting things from stunted personality traits to full-out psychosis of the Charles Manson variety. I don't want to frighten you unnecessarily, but if your lover ignores margins, has worryingly small handwriting that slants excessively in either direction, omits certain syllables, or has violently crossed Ts, you have more to worry about than what outfit you are going to wear when you meet.

So the next time you dismiss snail mail as being antiquated and irrelevant, think about how wonderful it would be to receive little tokens of affection in this age of immaterial intimacy. If that doesn't interest you, at least consider the handwriting, so you don't end up dating the next Ted Bundy.

THE LOVE POET

Professor Jonathan McDaniels found the little blue envelope tucked in his cubbyhole outside of the English department. He placed it on his desk and examined it carefully with a magnifying glass. Finding nothing out of the ordinary, he held the envelope briefly to his nose and then deposited it unopened into a folder marked 'extracurricular work'.

Over the years, McDaniels had received similar notes from infatuated students. Not once in all that time had he been tempted to take action, even as he watched his colleagues self-destruct before his eyes. They always gave the same excuses. They were tired. Tired of paperwork. Tired of indifferent students. Tired of reading the same boring essays that kept them from their own work, from dreams of novels and screenplays and fame. When had desire seeped through their fingers, ambition left to rot on the vine like forgotten fruit? Pretty girls at least offered some solace--payback for all those years of teaching students who would never appreciate their sacrifices.

A second note in the same blue paper arrived a week later. McDaniels placed it in the folder with the first, wondering if it was the budding poet with the crimson lips in his Intro to Shakespeare class. Perhaps it was the petite redhead in History of Romantic Poets, or the long-legged brunette in Gothic Fiction.

The third note arrived with no envelope. McDaniels picked it up gingerly and it opened on his desk like some trick lotus origami.

Let the honey words drip
between us
phrases of fluid peach
Pressed against the flesh of our mouths

It reminded him of a remedial composition class he'd taught some years back. All semester, his students complained, informing him how irrelevant poetry was to their lives. That is, until the professor explained how words could be used as an effective tool for seduction. Then they sprang to life: the whiners, the pranksters, the troublemakers. His class of misfits came alive as if a fire had been lit under their jaded little souls. Words had power, McDaniels told them. The right ones could bring a person to their knees. He urged them to experiment and be fearless. A good percentage of students ended up writing him poems that year.

He dug through 'Extracurricular Work" searching for the other two letters, bewildered to find his hands trembling.

Note 1: *Today, I caught a glimpse of you walking across the lawn, and although the ground was covered with frost and your breath came out in little snowy clouds, the sky promised spring.*

Note 2: *I am the dark thing you desire. Hidden between what cannot be said or written and what you keep secret.*

Did the letters contain a clue? What did they mean, 'could not be written'?

McDaniels should have reported them to the dean. Instead, he sandwiched the notes between the pages of Complete Works by Rimbaud. On the drive home, he repeatedly reminded himself that he had never (not once) paid attention to the misguided crushes of his students. He was a *conscientious* educator.

The fourth note was sent to his university email address anonymously. It contained one line in bold:

Don't worry. I will come to you.

No name or date or hint of how and when his love poet would materialize.

For the next few weeks, Professor McDaniels walked around campus in an embarrassing state of arousal, holding his briefcase in front of him like a shield to hide his erection. He was sixteen again, hopelessly in love with Shawn Peters. The back of his neck tingled, his fingertips pulsed, even his hair follicles vibrated. He could not remember the last time he had felt so energized.

During classes, he stared boldly at his students, searching out his poet from the sea of possibilities. He paid special attention to the prettier girls, calling on them purposefully so he could watch their lips move when he asked questions. Maybe it's a boy, he thought, restlessly sweeping the faces of his young men. I am one of you, he thought, watching his students mingling together after lectures. After all, what really separated them? A few measly decades? Was he not still a man?

McDaniels dug out his old Levis, proud he could still fit into them. He even changed his hairstyle, much to the surprise of his barber who had been cutting his hair the same way for the past twenty-two years. He ignored the amused looks and comments of staff and colleagues. The sky, the

SKY promised spring and his previously empty world was full of possibility.

After classes, he rushed to his cubbyhole and checked his email obsessively, but there were no further clues or letters. *I will come to you,* she said, but the days passed and his secret admirer did not materialise.

Almost as quickly as he'd been transformed into a love-struck teenager, the Professor turned into an old man. Autumn segued into winter and he felt every one of his years. Gone was the lightness of step and the blue jeans, replaced by heartburn, which he countered by chewing antacid tablets, sometimes chasing them with a swig of the scotch he kept in his desk drawer for emergencies.

It didn't take his students long to become suspicious of their teacher's manic moods. Usually, his effervescence attracted them and they vied for his time and attention. Now they sidestepped the desperate look in his eyes, crouching in their seats, refusing to contribute to discussions and leaving the lecture hall as soon as class was over.

Undaunted, McDaniels continued his search. But no matter what he did, no one looked back at him as if he were the '*dark thing they desired*'. More like the dark thing that must be avoided.

Perhaps the letters were nothing more than a juvenile prank, courtesy of his colleagues. Maybe they were the work of his wife, Margot. She was capable of orchestrating such a scene. Particularly, as she had always accused him of wanting to sleep with his students, despite his impeccable record proving otherwise.

"After all, that's how *we* met," she liked to remind him.

"How many times have we been through this? You were not one of my students."

"No, but I was *a* student. A fact you conveniently forget."

"The distinction is irrelevant, Margot. I did not behave with any impropriety. Remember, it was *you* who seduced me. I wanted to wait until you graduated."

"But you didn't, Jonathan."

"You're missing the point."

"No," she said, looking tragic. "As usual, you are."

One evening in December, while McDaniels was grading papers in his office, there was a knock on his door. "Go away," he shouted. "I'm not here." The knocking became more persistent. He opened the door to find a young woman in a short plaid skirt and a t-shirt that said *Ironic*.

"Sorry. I'm late," she said.

He took stock of her: black hair, green eyes, attractive. He didn't remember her in any of his classes. "Office hours are over," he told her, his speech slow from the scotch. "Come back tomorrow."

"Uh, I sent you a note saying I would come. Unless you want to reschedule?" she said, with a crooked smile that ate at his heart like corrosive acid.

It was his Love Poet. In the flesh. Months overdue but standing there calmly, looking for all the world like a vamp, a Louise Brooks enchantress, complete with 1920s hair and scarlet lipstick, waiting for him to say something.

"Office hours are over," McDaniels repeated, ushering her out and locking the door behind her. This time he didn't even bother pouring the scotch into his World's Greatest Professor coffee mug.

Two days later she appeared at his house.

"I wanted to explain about the other day. I know I upset you, but you didn't give me a chance to explain."

McDaniels froze. She was standing on his Welcome mat, looking even lovelier than she had in his office. A hundred fragmented thoughts passed through his brain, but he couldn't think of a single thing to say that would convey the terrible inappropriateness of what was happening.

"I couldn't come to see you before, but I wanted you to know that every word I wrote still stands."

McDaniels passed a hand over his hair, hoping the static wasn't audible. "This is unacceptable," he croaked.

"Let me explain," she wedged her foot in the doorway. "Can we talk about this inside?" She waited for a few moments. "Professor McDaniels, you have to say it. You have to invite me in."

McDaniels moved out of her way and walked to the kitchen, feeling as if something sharp was lodged into his chest. He hoped he wasn't having a heart attack. Imagine if she had to perform CPR on him? Imagine if she didn't know how.

"I like your house," she said, trailing behind him. "Lots of paisley."

"Thank you. My wife's tastes, I'm afraid."

The look in her eyes was enough to make his throat constrict.

She asked him where the bathroom was and was gone for several minutes. When he went to check on her, he found her stretched out in his bedroom.

"I hope you don't mind, Professor. I'm not feeling too well."

"Do you need an aspirin? Do you want me to call anyone?"

"I'll be fine. I just need to lie down for a little while. Is that okay?"

It wasn't, but what could he say? McDaniels stood by the foot of his bed, trying to ignore her skirt, which had hiked up, inviting him to feast on the soft expanse of her delicate flesh.

"This is a terrific bed," she said, nodding at the antique four-poster that Margo had spent a small fortune on.

"I don't sleep here," said McDaniels. "I have an orthopaedic mattress in the other room. I am more comfortable there, or on the floor. My back, you see."

"What a waste." She closed her eyes and stretched her limbs like a starfish.

McDaniels licked his lips and then immediately chastised himself, wondering how his entire persona could change in an instant, from respectable lecturer to lecher of young ladies.

"I love a firm mattress. The harder the better." She smiled that smile again. "Probably a good motto for most things. Wouldn't you agree?"

Before he could reply, she turned over on her stomach. "Do you mind if I test it out for bouncebility?"

"Pardon?"

"*Bouncebility Factor.* Technical term. Weeeee!" Headache forgotten, his love poet kicked off her shoes and sprung on the mattress.

McDaniels felt like Humbert Humbert, watching as her slender feet rose higher and higher on the makeshift trampoline. Free from self-conscious gravity or decorum, her backside and leg muscles uncoiled under her skirt, her limbs taut, smooth and endless.

"Come on. Join me." She held out her hand.

"Absolutely not," the Professor said, as if she had suggested he set fire to his marital bed.

"Why not?"

"Because beds are for sleeping, not for jumping. Now please stop, before you fall and hurt yourself."

Her dark hair rose and fell in rhythm.

"Don't you want to know my name or why I am here?"

He licked his lips again. He had a pretty good idea.

"N I N A. My name is Nina Parks."

"Fine. Please get off my bed, *Miss Parks*."

"I'm giving your bed 5 out of 5 stars," she said, pounding the mattress with relish. The bed coils squealed for mercy, and McDaniels clutched his chest and hoped his neighbours didn't come over to investigate.

"I was a cheerleader at school, you know. Look what I can do," she said, stretching her legs into an aerial split. "I'm a bird. I'm a plane. I'm Superman!"

She ran through a gamut of remarkable pretzel-like contortions, each more exotic than the last. Some which could only be described as gravitationally complex.

"I am going to have to insist that you stop now," McDaniels said, attempting to wrestle control.

"Look. What. I. Can. Do," Nina breathed, reaching behind her and unzipping her skirt. She hopped on one leg and then the other, never missing a beat.

"Stop that. What are you doing?" McDaniels said handing her the clothing she'd flung across the room.

His friends were wrong. He wasn't one bit like them. He wasn't a dirty old man frightened of death or aging, or whatever pathetic excuse they gave for taking advantage of girls a third their age. He had a sudden urge to ask her age.

"I'm not telling. Anyway, how old are you?"

"I'm not sure that's an appropriate question."

"Why not?"

McDaniels could not think of an appropriate response. "How old do you think I am?" he said instead.

"I don't care. Like they say, age doesn't mean a thing. Sixty-eight? Sixty nine?"

His heart reeled from the two-pronged attack of compliment and insult. "I'm sixty-four," he snapped. "Your turn."

"Over eighteen, if that's what you're concerned about." She bounced again.

McDaniels's emotions were spinning like a roulette wheel: guilt, pride, shame, lust and back again. He felt an aching desire to ignore it all and see her naked.

"Why are you frowning? Don't you find me attractive? Why are you turning away?" Nina stopped jumping.

"I find you attractive. Beautiful. But this is wrong."

"You don't remember me, do you?" she said in a quiet voice. "There was an article you wrote about romantic correspondence. It was a long time ago."

How could he forget? McDaniels had taken a sabbatical to work on his book of Victorian letters. *Victorian porn,* Margot called it. Unable to write, McDaniels had spent the summer locked in his office, reading the tantalizing letters of a woman named Sabine. Sweet, lovely Sabine. The erotic debauchery, the hours fantasizing about her letters, letters so hot, they practically seared his fingertips. He shredded each one, in case Margot found them, but not before he'd memorized every scintillating word. Sabine grew too attached. She insisted they meet. McDaniels, faithful to his ungrateful wife till the last, had to put a stop to their correspondence. It almost killed him. Years later, he could still recite every one of her letters.

How did Nina know about Sabine?

"Don't you remember me, Jonathan?"

He stared at her in shock. *She* was the secret referred to in her note. But that was over ten years ago. Sweet Jesus, had he been corresponding with Lolita? McDaniels took a deep breath, attempting to compose himself.

"I wrote you dozens of letters. I thought we had something, but you broke it off without an explanation."

"Listen, why don't you get dressed and meet me in the kitchen. I'll make us coffee."

"I can't believe you want to make me go away again. You have no idea how long I've been waiting for you. Do you know I applied to this school because you teach here? I sat in your classes, but you never noticed me. I thought if I sent you the letters you'd sent me, you'd remember."

Like a puzzle with its last piece in place, it finally clicked. Sabine/Nina wasn't writing him love letters, she was quoting lines he had written HER all those years ago. No wonder he was walking around like someone set him on fire. He'd remembered all her words but had forgotten his own, which, delicious irony, had come full circle to act as a noose – his own forbidden passion his undoing.

She leapt off the bed. "Jonathan."

He flinched. "Nina. Is that even your real name?"

She nodded.

"Look," he cleared his throat. "I am greatly flattered. My ego thanks you. But I'm afraid that is where it ends. This is inappropriate. You are my student. You should not be here in my house, half-undressed and on my bed. I am truly sorry about the letters. I had no idea. Unfortunately, I can't take back what I wrote. I can however, take responsibility for my actions from this point onward. If you decide to lodge a complaint or speak to someone in the department, I will support you one hundred percent."

"Why would I do that?" Nina said. "I don't want you to take back or apologise for anything you said."

"I can make an appointment with the Dean or a counsellor."

"Oh, Jonathan," she said. "You're such a prude. In a deliberate movement, without taking her eyes off him, she pulled her sweater over her head.

McDaniels' heart crashed against his ribcage and collapsed somewhere near his pelvic region.

"I behaved like an infatuated girl." She said, shrugging off the sleeves. "It took me a while to understand. It was a game. I didn't know how to play and my feelings were hurt.

But don't worry. I've learned a lot since then. I'm an adult now. A *consenting* adult."

She stepped daintily out of the remainder of her clothing, and then she stood gloriously naked in front of him. McDaniels could feel the heat of her emanating from her skin in waves.

"All things considered, I'd say we were years overdue for this."

"*Stop,*" he begged. "Miss Parks, Please, put your clothes back on."

Nina, like Venus incarnate, continued to stand poised before him, her cool shoulders and marble neck contrasting with the ripeness of her flesh. There were no traces of self-consciousness. She stood immobile, letting him have his fill of her.

He wondered how she could have sat in his classroom all this time, how he never noticed.

When Nina smiled, the illusion of perfection was shattered. No longer Venus, her mouth parted so the dark slashes of her lips revealed sharp little teeth.

He made one last feeble stab at resistance, but it was too late. She pressed her body against him and everything, from Nina's impossibly tiny waist, to the curve of her buttocks, was amplified, electric, in his arms. His ears roared. His head exploded. He leaned in and bit her, closing his eyes to better savour her salty sweetness.

McDaniels, stand-up man of letters, who had successfully kept dozens of infatuated students at bay, who had remained faithful to Margot, who had never strayed, not even once, refusing even the temptation of sweet Sabine, gave in to the vibrancy and danger of Nina's mouth, believing, or perhaps hoping, that at his age anything was possible, even absolution.

MATCH MADE IN HEAVEN

CHARLOTTE, EDITOR OF romance novels by day and die-hard anti-romantic the rest of the time, decided to try her hand at online dating. She waited until her husband Tom was asleep on the couch, before sneaking into his study to set up her profile. This being the early days of the Internet, cyber dating was still considered an odd and slightly dangerous undertaking, which gave it that extra titillating factor. She answered a few short questions about her preferences: sense of humour, lover of books, fan of sci-fi narratives, and then searched through an old shoebox of photos for something suitable. She opted for a Polaroid taken outside of the registry office where they were married, in what had to be the shortest ceremony in recorded history. In less time than it took to make a bowl of microwaved popcorn, a justice of the peace pronounced them man and wife.

"That's it?" she said, blinking at Tom.

"Don't worry," the judge said, shrugging off his black robes to reveal golf togs underneath. "It's legally binding. Don't forget to pay the cashier on the way out." And with a hasty wave, he rushed out of the room with his bag of clubs.

The picture was fuzzy, three-quarters of her body out of the frame. Charlie carefully photoshopped Tom from the other half and uploaded it to Match Made in Heaven.

"You realise you are a walking cliché," said her colleagues at Happily Ever After Books. "You own cats. You wear cardigans and sensible shoes. There's even a film about your life, starring Kathleen Turner."

"She was a romance writer," said Charlie. "I'm on the business end of things. Plus, I'm not looking to fall in love. I just want to meet someone who makes me laugh."

"You are setting the bar too low," everyone said, as they set her up with friends of friends of their husbands and boyfriends.

This was before she met Tom. Before everyone told her that spending her evenings eating microwave dinners and watching Star Trek: The Next Generation was a colossal waste of time.

Previously immune to that kind of criticism, she could no longer ignore her biological clock, which had commenced its own countdown. She discovered her first grey hair at 30. At 33, a set of tiny etchings appeared under her eyes. At 35, gravity began pulling at the corners of her lips, making her look as if she was perpetually frowning. Was this nature's way of letting her know that her romantic possibilities would soon become a barren wasteland? She saw a bleak future stretched out before her with nothing but her cats to keep her company, while everyone she knew fell in love, got married and had children.

Had all those years observing the love lives of other people ruined her chances for romance? On paper, Charlie was fearless, inquisitive, wisely choosing which books would appeal most to her audience. In reality, she couldn't even get a follow-up date.

"Nothing? Not one single call back?" her friends said, incredulous. "You are setting the bar too high. Dating is supposed to be *fun.* You need to loosen up. Let yourself go. Be light-hearted. Less demanding. You aren't talking about your cats, are you?"

One of them would inevitably Google Things You Should Not Talk About On A Date: sex/exes/religion/politics/jobs/diets/loneliness/health/babies/marriage/other blind dates/ and of course, pets.

What am I supposed to talk about? She wondered.

"Yourself, silly. Be yourself."

Charlie tried to listen attentively while her dates rambled on about their hobbies and ambitions. She smiled politely at their jokes. She even stuck to the index card of permissible topics.

"I have accepted the possibility that I may have to kiss the odd frog or two in hopes of triggering a spark where none exists," she said. "But I'm losing hope."

"Have faith," her friends said. "Your prince is out there somewhere."

Prince? At this point, Charlie would settle for someone she could go to the movies with.

Romance, the real kind as opposed to the fiction variety, was infinitely more complex than the pages she read every day. For starters, there were no gruff handsome strangers with six-packs and faraway eyes looking to sweep her away. And her bosom did not heave, not even once in all those blind dates.

Even as an adolescent, Charlotte had guarded herself from the possibility of romance. Hoping that being around other people her own age would bring her out of her shell, her parents signed her up for summer camp. Charlotte was miserable. She hated the enforced gaiety, the hikes, the tinny taste of well water. She couldn't relate to any of the girls, who weren't interested in making friends as much as they were desperate to pair off with boys. It was like something from the Discovery Channel. By the first week, kids were walking around two-by-two like animals from Noah's Ark—animals with fingers stuck in one another's jean pockets. They went around entwined at all times, reluctantly separating only at meals or to go to the bathroom.

"I can't really explain what it is like to be in love," said a blonde girl, as they stood in line at the canteen. "But it is like, you just know."

"Yeah," said another girl. "It's like me and Eddie. Love's a sickness," she said dreamily. "But like a *good* sickness. You feel all weird and like you have a fever? And you do silly things you wouldn't normally."

"Being in love is like surfing on a giant fluffy cloud," said a third girl. Everyone in line agreed. "Mine is so enormous I can't see anything else. It like blocks everything out."

"What, like the sun?" said Charlotte, who couldn't help joining in the conversation.

"Don't be daft," said the blonde girl, rolling her eyes. "That's not even like the same thing." She elbowed the other girls and they too rolled their eyes, leaving Charlotte in the line by herself.

One evening during campfire sing-a-long after a particularly off-key round of *Kumbaya*, a tall boy approached Charlotte.

I have something for you," he said, motioning her to follow him to a secluded place under the trees. "Hold out you hand."

When she refused, he took a deep breath. "It's a tree frog," he said, opening his palm.

Charlotte stared at the tiny amphibious creature and then at the boy, who had hazel eyes and so many freckles, they looked like constellations.

"I got it for you. *Especially*."

"But why?" she asked, unable to see how the slimy thing related to her in any way.

The boy looked at his shoes for a few seconds and then grinned at her. "Cause you are as ugly as a toad," he said, sticking out his tongue. He sauntered back to his group of giggling friends.

That night Charlotte sat on the campfire log until all the campers had left and the embers died out. She didn't understand how a group of idiot boys were anything like a cloud. What did girls see in them? Was the camp serving some sort of goofy love potion along with the kool-aid? And if so, why didn't she get any?

At the end of the eight weeks, the campers clung to one another in a flood of tears, saliva and promises, making Charlotte glad she'd remained disentangled from the messiness of teenage romance. She promised herself that when it came time to fall in love, she'd do so quietly and with dignity.

But in high school and later, college, the same pattern emerged, her friends needing only the slightest commonality before hurling themselves lemming-like into relationships. *You like soup? What a coincidence. I LOVE soup!* Her classmates were so naive and eager, so desperate to grab on to the coattails of romance at every opportunity.

It was like a nature programme she'd once watched on television. When it came time for mating season, the salmon would go to extraordinary lengths: swim upstream, travel for thousands of miles, do whatever it took to find a mate. *Any* mate. Fish, like her classmates, apparently had no criteria when it came to love.

Later, as adults, when hormones could no longer be held responsible, her friends continued behaving as if romance were something mystical involving the stars and planets.

"Charlie," said her colleagues. "How are you going to find someone if you always play it safe? You don't take risks.

You don't let yourself fall. Close your eyes and take a leap, you might just be surprised at where destiny leads you."

She wanted to tell them that destiny had nothing to do with falling in love. Finding someone was a combination of being in the proper mind-set and standing at the crossroads of right time and place. How could her friends, smart, independent women who didn't normally believe in fairy tales, be so illogical when it came to relationships? And why was common sense at such extreme odds with desire? A good-looking man was one thing. Wanting destiny to make the big decisions was the stuff of teenage fantasy.

Despite her occupation, or perhaps because of it, Charlotte had heard more tales of failed romances than of happily ever afters. She'd spent hundreds of hours listening to colleagues and friends recount break-ups, replaying endless details, as they lay on the analytical couch of self-regret. "I don't understand what went wrong. We seemed so right for each other."

Invariably, someone would repeat the mantra. "Don't Worry. One day you'll find someone worthy of you," as if finding a suitable partner was an exercise in blind faith, not common sense.

Charlotte selected a black and white photo taken in Paris.

Tom wanted the Grand Canyon, but she had already bought tickets.

Paris: the city of lights. The city of romance and countless possibilities. Could there be a more perfect place?

Charlotte had never looked forward to anything as much as that trip. She read travel books. She bought a Toulec Le trouc poster and hung it in the kitchen. She made a to-do list of all the things she'd do with Tom: walk hand-in-hand along the Seine, kiss on the Pont Neuf Bridge, stay in bed drinking wine and feeding one another grapes. It didn't matter that Tom didn't even like grapes.

When they checked into their hotel after a fourteen-hour flight, the only room available was a single with twin beds. The jet-lagged couple trudged four flights of stairs with their suitcases to find themselves in a space slightly bigger than a closet. "I don't understand," Charlotte said. "The brochure said we had a view of the Eiffel Tower."

"Obviously, we don't," snapped Tom, unpacking his toiletries and placing them on the tiny sink. "We could have had a spectacular view of the Canyon but *you* insisted on Europe. He climbed into one of the beds and was asleep within minutes.

This was not what she had imagined when dreaming of Paris. The next morning, she woke late to find a note on her bedside table. *"Didn't want to disturb you. Went to the Louvre. Back later. Tom."*

Charlotte wondered how her life could be so devoid of romance. But it was not in her nature to brood. If romance hadn't yet made an appearance, it was up to her to invite it in. Sitting up, she reached for a magazine she'd found on the plane. Page 39 promised: TOP TEN TIPS GUARANTTED TO DRIVE HIM MAD WITH DESIRE, focusing on No.4. *Sexy Makeovers and Glamour Shots.* The accompanying photo showed a leggy blonde reclining in a four-poster bed wearing a pair of stilettos and little else.

In her pair of silver sandals and matching set of lingerie bought especially for the trip, she posed experimentally, imagining what Tom would say when he saw the photos. But when he came in a few minutes later, holding a map and a baguette, he did a dramatic double take like a cartoon character.

"What on earth are you doing with my camera?" was all he managed, as he stared at his wife crouching over the bed.

Charlotte sat up, trying to cover herself with the sheet. "I was posing. For a photo. Sexy glamour shots," she stammered.

Tom marched over and removed the pillowcase draped over the bedside lamp. "That's a fire hazard, Charlotte." He returned the lamp to its rightful place on his side of the room. Avoiding her eyes, he picked up the baguette he'd brought, jabbing it in her direction. "I thought you might be hungry."

"Wait," Charlotte said. But it was too late. Her husband rushed out the door before she could explain and didn't return till later that evening.

Tom appeared like a godsend—a Star Trek forum to be precise. A place Charlotte could be herself and not care whether anyone saw her grey hairs or wrinkles.

She and Tom found common ground in the adventures of Captain Kirk and in a mutual love of Thai green curry. Like her, Tom disliked small talk and preferred science fiction to comedies. He was smart and engaging and could recite every single episode of Dr. Who.

One late night, after chatting for five hours, he told her he was sick of meeting women with whom he had nothing in common. He had almost lost hope that this ideal woman even existed. That is, until now.

"I'd like to go out with you. On a proper date," he told her.

Charlotte felt a not together unpleasant pressure in her ribcage. This must be the onset of what everyone called *love*—an amalgamation of gratitude, relief and giddiness. Like receiving a long anticipated present she'd specifically requested on her birthday.

"I met someone," she told her colleagues one Monday afternoon. "His name is Tom. He's 34. He works in IT."

"Charlie, that's wonderful! Spill the beans. We want details. How did you two meet?"

"We met online."

"On an e-dating site?" The teachers exchanged looks.

"On a science fiction forum actually. There was a discussion about the importance of the Enterprise in space exploration and Tom was very eloquent in his defence. As it turns out, we have a lot in common," Charlotte said, taking a bite of her sandwich.

"Why online, though? We set you up with quite a few attractive, eligible men and you end up with some guy you met on your computer."

"I'm sorry, I appreciate all your help in finding me a date, but I'm not very good at meeting new people. I was always so worried about whether I was making a good impression that I could never relax and be myself. I don't feel that way with Tom. He's easy to talk to. He gets me. I get him."

"To each his own," her friends said. There were several minutes of silence, as everyone ate their lunches. "So you two have met? This compatibility exists in person?"

"I'm not sure," said Charlotte. "We're going on our first date next week." She knew her friends would react this way, which is why she had delayed telling them.

"How long ago did you say you first met?"

"Almost two months ago."

"Are you kidding? And you still haven't met?"

"I didn't want to rush into anything. Besides, we're still getting to know one another."

"By discussing what television shows you like?"

"What's wrong with that?"

"It's a romance killer, that's what! He should be taking you out to dinner. Or dancing. Otherwise, how will you ever know?"

"Know what?"

"Come on, don't be so naïve," her colleagues said. You have to find out if you have *chemistry*. You plan on having sex with this guy, right?"

Charlotte wrapped her half-eaten sandwich and brushed the crumbs carefully from her lap.

"Charlotte."

"It isn't about sex. I'm happy just chatting. Tom is fun. Neither of us is in a rush to get physical."

"Well that sounds more like a friend than a boyfriend."

"He's definitely not just a friend."

"How would you know?"

"I just do. And the other stuff will kick in later. I'm not worried."

Three months later, Charlotte took a bus to the city courthouse with a copy of her birth certificate and married Tom in a quickie civil ceremony. Despite her hopes, marriage didn't turn out the way she had hoped, and if Charlotte didn't do something, the disappointment would eat away at her bones until there was nothing of her but exhaled sadness.

Charlotte peered at the black and white Paris photo. Part of her face was cast in shadow and it was blurry, but it had a Catherine Deneuve in *Belle de Jour* quality.

She tiptoed into the living room to make sure Tom was still asleep. After ten months of marriage, her husband was already behaving as if they had been together for twenty years. His head was flung back and there was drool pooled on the left side of his mouth.

Charlotte considered wiping it off. Instead, she went back into the office and uploaded her photo to Match Made in Heaven. Under status she firmly checked 'single'.

SPACE COWBOY

THOMAS HARDAWAY STOOD in his office clenching his hands and holding his breath. When he felt anxious, his doctor told him, he should remember to breathe and stay calm, but then his doctor didn't have to work with Brian Norman, AKA Dbrain.

Thomas explained to his underling for the tenth time that 'Casual Friday' referred to relaxed office attire, not a call for unprofessional demeanor. Dbrain, as usual, wasn't listening. He was sitting on top of Thomas' desk, shoving his laptop into his face.

"T-Man, check her out. Crazy hot or what?"

The crazy hot female in question was a slim brunette in a pencil skirt. She was smiling at the camera, unaware that her photo would soon be circulating the IT department.

"I told you," said Thomas, through gritted teeth. "You can't be uploading people's photographs without their permission. Now delete that and get off my desk. And please stop calling me T-Man."

"Not until you examine this fine, rare specimen. T—oops, my good man, this is 100 percent, prime choice, top quality female. A firm contender for second, maybe even first place on my Top Ten List."

While other employees spent their productive hours choosing fantasy sports teams, Dbrain's favorite pastime consisted of compiling a league table of co-workers, office temps and cute waitresses from the TGI Fridays down the road. For weeks a shapely redhead from HR reigned undefeated. A redhead Dbrain swore was the carbon copy of the woman from *Mad Men*.

"Brian, stop drooling over my screen. It's perverse."

"It's not like she can see me."

"Yes, but *I* can see you." Thomas felt one of his migraines coming on and fumbled in his desk drawer looking for his medication. His co-worker would lick the dirty floor if a pretty girl asked him to. Make that *any* girl.

"Go upstairs and deal with Robertson's computer. He's been calling all morning."

"But I'm busy."

"Brian, you have ten seconds to get your rear off my desk or I'm writing you up."

"Fine, fine. I'm going." Dbrain brushed his lips against the laptop once more for good measure. "You know what?" he said, seating himself at his desk. "This chick is officially hotter than my *numero uno*."

"Don't refer to women as *chicks*. She has a name, you know."

"Sure, sure. Whatever, T-Man. Don't you think New Girl looks just like Megan Fox?"

"No."

"She does where it counts."

"Please get back to work."

"I *am* working. I'm uploading her to the Intranet." Dbrain opened a spreadsheet, inserting the new girl's name at the top. "What do you think? Uptight? Sweet? Quiet? It says here she's a freelance consultant. What do you think she consults? She doesn't look like the numbers type."

"Why, because she isn't wearing dorky glasses and holding a calculator?"

"LOL," said Dbrain.

That was another quirk of Brian's that made Thomas want to shoot him. He closed his eyes and ignored the flash of bright light behind his left eyeball. He had explained over one hundred times that 'LOL' was an acronym you wrote, not uttered. Dbrain had looked at him blankly and then said how about *ROFL?*

"I wonder if she has a Facebook account? Bang. She certainly does. Along with 230 photos—all available to the general public. Come to papa, Megan. Come to papa."

"You can do that during your lunch break. We need to get back to work."

Dbrain ignored him, but for once Thomas had to admit that he was right. From his desk, he could see her Facebook photos, each more gorgeous than the last. She made the other women in his office seem plain in comparison. Not that Thomas saw much of his fellow co-workers. Stuck in the basement, he rarely saw anyone, except the janitor, the mail clerk and fucking Dbrain.

When he was offered a job at Innotech, complete with his own office and junior tech, Thomas was thrilled. That is, until he discovered that his office, next to the servers and discarded office equipment, was so tiny, he kept passing it, thinking it was the supply closet. His junior tech, knew almost nothing about computers, except how to surf the Net and send emails. When Thomas asked Brian if had any hobbies, he replied with a straight face that he was an expert in the art of the female subtext. Thomas had initially been intrigued by this comment, until he realized that Dbrain thought subtext meant the funny comments people posted under their photos in Facebook.

"You see, T-Man, they leave their permissions open for a *reason*."

"It's called inexperience. I'm sure if they knew some bored IT geek was spending all day drooling over their summer holiday snaps, they'd wise up and lock you out."

"See? That proves you don't get it. They *want* people to look."

"Let's agree to disagree. Now are you finished with all the projects on your to-do list?"

"About that. See, I don't get why we have to bust our humps," Dbrain stopped fiddling with his spreadsheet and looked at Thomas. "We fix things. The morons break them again. We fix them and they call us a few days later. It's a never-ending cycle. I don't see the point."

"Brian, remember last week when we had our one-to-one? We agreed that you would not waste company time arguing about your responsibilities. Also, you are not to refer to your co-workers as *morons*."

"It's difficult, when they're always nagging me: *why has the computer eaten my spreadsheet? Why do I have a virus? Is it because technology doesn't like me?* Yeah, that's right, jerk-off. Technology *hates* you."

Thomas slowly counted to ten. "You do realize it is our job to help them? That's why they hired us. We are troubleshooters. Those 'jerks', as you refer to them, don't know how to pinpoint the problem themselves."

"So now we're supposed to think for them too?"

"Of course not. But at the same time you can't go around deleting people's files because they ignored you in the cafeteria."

"That wasn't me. That was poetic justice or karma or whatever. Listen, T-Man. You don't know what these people are like. It's high school all over again. The pretty girls only talk to you when they need help with something and the jocks want to abuse you publicly to impress the girls."

At times, Thomas almost felt sorry for Dbrain. He knew what it was like to have people treat you a certain way because of your looks. Even as a child, Thomas had invited ridicule with his nerdy, oversized glasses, unruly hair that parted to one side, no matter what he did with it, and his unfashionable wardrobe, courtesy of his mother, who insisted that girls liked boys who wore sweater vests.

At university, girls stopped ignoring him and sat next to him in lectures and afterward invited Thomas out for coffee. It was only after they asked for his help with computer programs, class assignments and printer/copy machine issues that he understood the purpose behind all the attention. Thomas didn't take it personally. Having spent his life as the resident nerd, he was used to being ignored, used and beaten up, sometimes all of the above. He decided to take the high road and not let girls make him feel petty and foolish. As long as he didn't take the pseudo invites seriously, everything would be fine. Thomas even managed to make his appearance work for him, getting a job at university as a computer tech, reasoning that if people were going to approach him for help, he ought to be paid for it.

On days when he didn't feel generous, he found ways to get back at the manipulative girls, such as 'accidentally' deleting their term papers minutes before they had to be handed in. It served them right for being stupid and not understanding the importance of saving their documents.

The staff at Innotech treated him with respect and courtesy. Of course it was a different era now: the era of the geek, when it was smart to be nice to the guy in charge of your Internet and email. Thomas would never do something like that to one of his co-workers but it went without saying that he could seriously mess with their lives if he felt like it.

That was the difference between having genuine power and abusing it. Brian would do well to learn from him.

"Look at it this way," Thomas said. "Who rules the world? Neanderthals or nerds?"

"Mark Zuckerberg, that's who."

"Yes, you are partially right. It certainly isn't some chiselled-chin jerk in Marketing. Geeks hold all the knowledge and therefore the power. If we wanted, we could be destructive and hold a grudge, but we're better than that. We have ethics."

"Right on, T-Man. Geeks like us totally rule the planet."

Thomas had not included him in his magnanimous speech. Dbrain, despite his nickname, didn't have much going on upstairs. He didn't have much going on anywhere else either. He had the misfortune of looking like a nerd, with the subzero brain power of a jock. Dbrain was always talking himself up as an expert in something or other, but the truth was that he was average. An average expert of the social media generation, who knew how to turn on a computer, text on his mobile phone and talk a lot of nonsense.

Later that afternoon, Thomas looked up from his computer and standing before him was the same woman who earlier had been dancing on Dbrain's monitor as a screen saver, her head superimposed on the body of Jessica Alba. Not that she needed any help in the body department.

"IT Department, right? Am I in the right place?"

Thomas cleared his throat but Dbrain beat him to the punch. "IT gurus. That's us. What can I do to sort you out?"

Thomas had to stop himself from physically attacking Brian. He stood, blinking back the stabbing pain in his temporal lobe. "Peabody on seventh is having printer problems, can you assist?" He turned to the brunette. "I'll help you," he said.

She walked over to his desk and picked up his nameplate. "Head of Information Technology. Impressive. Sorry I didn't make an appointment. I thought I'd come down here and introduce myself personally. Don't you just hate it when people bounce emails around endlessly?"

Thomas, who preferred people to do exactly that, nodded his head in agreement. Usually he found it hard to maintain eye contact, but he couldn't stop staring. Her eyebrows in particular were intriguing. Dark and delicately arched, one of them positioned a few centimeters higher than the other. He wondered if she'd plucked them that way or if nature had styled them.

"So, what do you need from me?" she said, crossing her legs and smiling at him.

A slew of messages appeared on Thomas' screen.

BN: What are you doing looking at her forehead?

BN: Look at her skirt! She's totally doing a Sharon Stone.

BN: I bet you she's not wearing any panties.

BN: Get a good eyeful and remember all the details so can tell me later.

BN: Man, don't make me come over there and show you how it is done.

Thomas slammed his laptop shut.

"Is everything okay?" she asked.

"Yes. My computer froze. I'll reboot."

She uncrossed her legs, stood up and went to stand near Thomas' desk. If this were anyone else, he would have hit the roof and told them to return to their seats and let him do his job. The thing was, she smelled good. Better than good. Intriguing and sweet at the same time. When she walked into the office it was one of the first things he noticed, her unusual scent of warm sunshine, honey and leather. He took a discreet whiff and then another, each time smelling a different thing. But the fragrance was closing in on his lungs and he was having difficulty breathing. Steady. Keep calm, Thomas told himself, trying not to panic. Keep inhaling and exhaling. But his haphazard wheezing was audible, even to his own ears, his lungs sounding like defective bagpipes.

"Are you all right?" she said, looking concerned as Thomas went pale and then bright red.

"Fine," he gasped, hunting around his pockets for his inhaler. Where had he put it? Oh, that's right. Dbrain had been playing with it earlier, pretending it was a transponder and he was Captain Kirk.

"Sorry. Have. To. Finish. This. Later." He rushed out of his office and down the corridor.

Thomas lay very still on the cool marble floor of the bathroom and tried to meditate the way Dr. Hang had advised, until his lungs stopped contracting. Asthma attacks were not uncommon, but Thomas had never freaked out in front of anyone from IBP. Those days of being bullied and ridiculed were behind him. He prided himself on being professional and competent. The guy who could solve any problem. Now she was going to think that he was a loser like Brian, falling over himself all because a pretty girl had stood next to him.

After ten minutes, he stood up and took a sip of water directly from the tap. He would simply apologize for running away. Apologize and tell her he was getting over an illness. Maybe a stomach bug. Or was that too graphic? Better stick to some sort of generic malaise.

"Where did she go?" he asked when he returned to his desk.

Brian was staring intently at his screen. "Huh?"

"The woman who was here a few minutes ago. The one on your screensaver? Where did she go?"

"I think she said something about being late for a meeting."

Thomas sank into his chair. He thought about sending her an email and then bristled when he realized she didn't have an email account. That's why she had come to see him in the first place. "Did she happen to say anything about setting up an account?"

"Yeah, as a matter of fact she did," said Dbrain. "But don't worry. I took care of it."

"What?"

"That's SOP, right?"

"Brian, please don't use acronyms when you're speaking."

"Standard. Operating. Procedure."

"Thank you. Now please tell me you didn't do what we talked about you not doing."

"Hey, no. I don't do that anymore. Stop looking at me like that. I didn't do anything. Don't you trust me?"

"Not particularly."

"Nice, T-Man. Way to diss a *mate*. He pronounced 'mate' in the style of Crocodile Dundee. You know what? I've had enough abuse for the day. I'm going out for a soda. I'd ask if you wanted one, but since you don't trust me, you can forget it."

Dbrain mumbled something else under his breath that did not sound complimentary but Thomas let it go, making a mental note to mention his behaviour at their next evaluation. He waited until he heard the elevator move before walking over to Dbrain's desk. He wasn't sure what he was looking for but he was familiar with his tech's SOP when it came to female colleagues.

Brian liked to go into what he called his 'Boo Radley mode'—a more helpless and dim-witted version of his usual self, strategically designed so women would feel sorry for him. Blushing and stuttering, he asked them all manner of personal questions they would normally not give out. Incredibly, seven out of ten times they gave him what he wanted.

When Thomas first witnessed this party trick, he couldn't believe anyone was naïve enough to give out details in this day and age. Especially as knowledge in the hands of an idiot like Dbrain, amounted to a dangerous thing.

"That's the geek's double-edged sword. They may not lust after us, but they always trust us. And trust, as you know, T-Man, equals power. As you keep saying we are the *Problem Solvers.*"

"Brian, stop making us sound like a cartoon duo. First of all, what you are doing is morally reprehensible. Second, it can get you fired. You can't hack into people's accounts."

"It is not strictly hacking, per se. They told me their passwords of their own free will."

"And what are you doing with that information?"

At this point, Brian would shrug, refusing to meet Thomas' eye.

"Is it my fault they're clueless? You'll never catch me giving someone my password."

"Listen to me. This is serious. If I ever see you doing it again, I will drag you to personnel myself to file a complaint. Don't make me do it."

"Fine. Calm down. It's not like I was taking money from their bank accounts. I'm just peeking at one or two emails, that's all."

"I don't want to hear another word about this, Brian. You are to cease stalking the employees of this company. Understand?"

For the tenth time that day, Thomas contemplated a world without Dbrain. He was still shaky from his asthma attack, but managed to calm down enough to see a clear and perfect solution in front of him. He loved when his mind went to blank screen like that, allowing everything else to float in the background while he focused on the main event.

He logged into his computer with his super admin account. The Finger of God, he called it, not that he believed in a higher deity. And why should he? Having ultimate power to everyone's computers, to browse through their many files and documents, accessing every byte of information, including that of his sneaky little underling, was the equivalent of being omnipotent. And anyway, he was Brian's boss. He was only checking that his underling was doing things by the book.

Thomas was rewarded minutes later by an electronic note on Brian's to-do list, written not long after the brunette was in the office. 'Item 5: new girl, aka Kallioppe likes chatting in virtual environments. Check out Second Life.'

As information went, it wasn't much, but it was enough.

That night, Thomas hunted for them both online. He was certain that wherever Dbrain was, he'd find her too. *Quid pro quo, Brian. Quid pro quo.* See how you like someone following you around.

***

Max was the nickname Thomas decided to use. 'Max' was the kind of person women found irresistible. Half misunderstood genius, half sensitive boy-man, he was the prototypical, motorcycle jacket wearing, cigarette flicking rebel. Max knew just the right way to hunch his shoulders while uttering catch phrases sure to ignite female libidos. Max played it cool. Max was hard to get, by turns aloof and cruel.

He waited for people to catch on to the fact that his dark hero was composed of stolen lines and gestures from old 50s films. Instead, he received a slew of emails, phone numbers, and personal messages with scorching invitations. He couldn't understand it. If he tried anything like that outside of the Internet, people would laugh at him—possibly even chase him out of town with pitchforks. But cockiness fit Max like a well-worn pair of biker boots.

He was only after one person. Only she was worth all the trouble. And Max, being the kind of cool antihero that he was, bid his time and waited for her to notice him.

***

For the first time in his life, Thomas' work went uncompleted. Like Brian, he was distracted by his personal projects, ignoring the piling help desk requests and emails. When not online, he spent his time prowling the fifth floor, hoping to catch a glimpse of her. Sometimes, he would hide behind the office plants and listen in as she traded jokes with the staff. Thomas pictured himself, stopping by her desk, casually inquiring about her weekend. He would be friendly but not too forward, the same as anyone. He might even tell her a funny anecdote. But whenever she looked his way, Thomas' throat tightened and he felt as if he were going to choke. His body—his stupid, clumsy body—betrayed him at every turn.

***

When Max finally found Kallioppe, he was relieved that she was the kind of outspoken independent woman who wasn't waiting around to be rescued, because let's face it, he didn't know how to rescue anyone, not even himself. She didn't pretend, which he found incredibly refreshing. She laughed when she was supposed to laugh and asked questions at all the right intersections. But somewhere behind Kallioppe's outspoken façade, there was a hint of the loneliness that Thomas understood better than anyone. It was as if she was sending him messages in a personal code only he could read. With her, time took on a fluid quality, hours passed like minutes. When she had to go, Max's insides compressed with sadness. Four hours of conversation weren't enough. Six hours, seven hours. Not enough. He raced home after work to talk to her. He fell asleep on his keyboard at dawn, and woke up to go back to work, with her on his mind. There was no finite point to his desire, which was both frightening and exhilarating, contrary to everything he thought relationships were supposed to be.

***

"You're different," said Dbrain.

"What do you mean, *different?*" said Thomas.

"I don't know. You sit at your computer all day long, staring at your screen. You don't tell me off anymore like you used to. You don't eat. You look like you haven't slept in weeks. What's up, T-Man?"

"Nothing. I just have a lot going on. Do you mind? I have work to do."

"I know what it is," Dbrain said, snapping his fingers. "It's a chick, right? Ha. You have it bad my friend and that ain't good."

"What is that supposed to mean?" Thomas asked, removing his glasses and rubbing his eyes. "Please stop being so cryptic."

"T-Man, don't you think I know? I may be a player but I understand women." He sat on the edge of Thomas' desk, playing with his Apollo 13 model until Thomas made him put it down.

"Chicks make you feel all soft and warm and cherished and shit, one minute, then they look at you like you're a useless worm. No, I take that back. A maggot writhing in a trashcan."

"Brian have you been licking mushrooms again?"

"Don't worry. It happens to the best of us. Your insides feel like they're going to fall out. But you have to keep it together. Get back to being your crusty no nonsense self."

"Thank you for the pep talk. I've got a report to write."

"Ok, but do we get each other?" Dbrain vaguely indicated a part of his nether region.

"What, your penis? How is that relevant?"

"Not that. Pride, man. That's what important. That's the whole point of being a man, understanding like, our purpose in the world. Don't let some girl, no matter how cute, take your pride from you."

In the past Thomas would have agreed one hundred percent. He hated people who fed on sweetness like lovesick vampires. But Thomas' love wasn't weak. It was vicious. Tenacious. Like plant life. It pulled itself out of the ground, uprooting everything in its path in a bid to ensure its own survival.

Humans were like plants. When it came down to it, they were willing to do anything to ensure their survival, even if that meant sacrificing an arm or a hand for the greater good of the cause. Dbrain had no idea what he was talking about. Pride no longer occupied a central place in Thomas' life. It sat backstage to his enormous anaconda-at-his-windpipe knot of fucked up guilt and love.

He was going to tell Kallioppe the truth but he was afraid about how she'd react when she found out he wasn't Max. Thomas had a feeling she would eventually understand why he had lied. Still, he kept delaying the confession, promising to tell her the next day, or the day after that, until his desire for honesty became blurred by his need for self-preservation.

Big fat worm indeed.

"Get back to work, Brian," he snapped.

***

When Thomas was a little boy, he spent most of his childhood under the dining room table, which doubled as a spaceship. Even at the age of three, he found other people an intrusion. He enjoyed his solitude, preferred it even. Except for his mother, the only person allowed to accompany him on his missions. Eileen would crawl under the table on her hands and knees to act as Thomas' co-pilot, implicitly understanding her role in her son's life. He wanted her there to guide him from impending dangers, such as meteors that might unknowingly sideswipe them as they sped around the galaxy. His mother understood why he refused to make friends with the boys at his school. She appreciated that he was a loner. A Space Cowboy, not one of those sad-faced children who longed desperately for the approval of others.

***

"Hey, IT guy, how's it going?" she said a few days later, appearing at his office with a cup of coffee from the vending machine.

"What are you doing here?" Thomas said, hoping she didn't notice his trembling voice.

Before she could say anything, Brian over went to greet her. "You ready to go?" he asked.

"He's helping me with some Internet problems I'm having at home," she said by way of explanation. "I would have asked you, but you're never in your office. We're going to lunch. You want to come with?"

Thomas shook his head, not trusting himself to speak.

"Would you like us to bring you back something? A sandwich or a salad?"

"Don't worry about T-man, he's not big into eating lately," said Brian, giving him a thumbs up as they out.

Thomas chewed two extra-strength painkillers, wishing he had a bottle of scotch to wash them down with. Max would have. He was the kind of guy to keep a bottle in his drawer. Maybe even two bottles. Max would have leaned against the vending machine, all cool and aloof, not bothered in the slightest that his girl was going out with the office nitwit. Max would have tagged along to lunch and then dazzled her with his smarts, making Dbrain look like a horse's ass. Max would have punched his Junior Tech right in the face.

Thomas always believed that when he found the right girl things would be effortless between them. Smooth. They would move from conversation to flirtation, perfectly paced, as if dancing a tango. But he couldn't even utter a word, clamming up whenever she spoke to him and making a fool of himself.

"Where were you?" he said to Dbrain, when his co-worker staggered back two hours later.

"Sorry. I lost track of time. I went for a walk after lunch to clear my head."

"Clear your head?" said Thomas, a darkness to his voice that he attributed to his alter ego.

"Yeah. It was a genuine mistake. It won't happen again."

"Damn right." He said standing over Dbrain's chair. "As of this moment you are no longer part of Innotech. I've been putting up with your lackadaisical attitude for too long. You don't listen. You don't care about helping anyone. You complain constantly about everything. Let's face it Brian, you are ill-suited to work at this company. Your IT skills are sub par."

"Are you kidding?" Dbrain gave him a hurt look. "All because I was a little late coming back?"

"Did you not hear everything else I said? This isn't working. I'm afraid I'm going to have to let you go."

Thomas had dreamed about this day for months. He had planned out how he'd say it, restraining himself from dancing and hopping around the office, but watching his crestfallen colleague took some of the joy out of the act.

"But it's Christmas, T-man."

"See? You can't even get that right. I tell you and tell you over again and still you don't listen. My name is THOMAS."

"OK, *Thomas*. You got me. I didn't go for a walk. I was doing some last minute shopping and I got you this." Dbrain looked sheepish as he pulled a package out of his jacket and put it on his desk. It was a silver astronaut on a key ring.

"Since you're all into space and stuff."

Thomas put the key ring on the desk without looking at it. "Yeah, well, it doesn't change a thing. You'll finish out your two weeks and we'll pay you for whatever time you have left. I've set up a meeting with personnel tomorrow."

Brian looked at him but didn't say a word. He just nodded and then sat hunched over his desk for the rest of the afternoon. For once in his life he was completely silent. He left at five on the dot without saying goodbye.

***

Thomas would have loved to skip the office Christmas lunch, but it was a mandatory event. In past years he'd gone and enjoyed himself. One year he'd even participated in the karaoke, belting out Bon Jovi's Livin' On A Prayer to the cheers of his colleagues.

His boss had called early that morning, reminding him that both he and Dbrain were expected at the restaurant at noon.

Dbrain was silent on the drive over, even as Thomas tried to make small talk. "If you don't mind, I'd rather we kept things formal," he said.

A large group was already seated at a special table in the back. *She* looked up and smiled, as a red-faced Thomas, ignoring the empty seat beside her, squeezed himself between the HR redhead (who most definitely did not look like the woman from *Mad Men*) and Ron, a marketing executive.

"How are my favorite IT guys?" he said shaking hands.

"Fine, fine," Thomas lied, as he watched Dbrain taking the seat next to the brunette.

"Champagne?" she asked.

"Great," Brian said. "I've had a lousy week. But I have a feeling it's going to get a whole lot better."

Thomas wished he hadn't brought him along to the Christmas lunch, requirement or no requirement. It dawned on him that Dbrain, refilling his glass with more champagne, was no longer part of the company, and now had nothing to keep him in check.

"We've been talking about online romances," the redhead, called Imogene said. "You guys must know all about that."

"Why, because we're geeks?" asked Dbrain.

"No, because I read in an article that next to being setup by friends, it is now the most popular way to meet people."

"Really?" Ron asked. Imogene quoted the respectable paper that had printed the statistic, but still no one seemed to believe there was any truth in it.

"How about you Thomas? You believe in online dating?" said Ron, grinning, as if he already knew the answer.

Thomas shook his head and checked to see if anyone had sent him a text message. He could feel the edges of panic gathering in his chest, the shortness of breath coming on.

Dr. Hang had suggested various relaxation exercises. "Go to a safe place where the air is fresh and clean," the doctor said, suggesting he revisit that scene from *The Sound of Music*, but Thomas hated musicals and being in the outdoors usually made his asthma worse.

"T-man isn't much into dating, online or off. He's too busy trying to save the world one byte at a time," Brian said. "He's practically a cyborg."

Everyone laughed. Everyone but her. "There is nothing wrong with that," she said in a quiet voice. "The world needs more superhero geeks."

"How about you," Brian asked her. "You into online dating?

She nodded, taking a sip of wine.

"Seriously? I would never have pegged you as one of those," said Ron.

"Why not? It is so much more romantic and safer than meeting someone at a bar. Chatting is fun. You should try it sometime."

"No thanks. I've heard horror stories about the kind of women you meet on there," he replied with a grimace.

"Oh, do tell," said Imogene.

"A person I know at my gym spent weeks chatting up someone he thought was the love of his life. Was even planning on leaving his partner for her, if you could believe it. So they met and *she* turned out to be a *he*."

"Get out of town," said Brian.

"True story."

Brian laughed and drained his glass. "So, did your friend go through with it anyway?"

"Of course not," said Ron. "But that's the whole fallacy of online dating. You can't trust what you don't see."

"You think seeing someone makes them more trustworthy? People deceive one another, get divorced, lie and cheat in person. You think you know someone, but you never know them completely. Let's face it," said Thomas. "Most people are untrustworthy online or off." It was the first thing he had said all afternoon and everyone stopped eating and looked at him.

"Well put. Which is why we have to take our chances where we get them," said Kallioppe, giving him a little wink.

"Hear, hear," said Ron.

"To love in the 21st century," they cheered, clinking their glasses.

"So, do you have an online boyfriend?" Brian asked Kallioppe.

"I don't like to kiss and tell."

"Where's the fun in that?" Brian said.

"There is one person I've been chatting to a lot recently."

Don't say it. Don't say it, thought Thomas.

"A mysterious guy who goes by the name Max, although I don't think that's really his name."

"What does this Max do?"

She shrugged. "All I know is that he's a rebel without a cause. I'm a sucker for guys like that."

"Have you met him yet?" asked Ron.

"Nope. And I don't think we ever will. Ours is purely a virtual thing. I have a real boyfriend."

"And does he know about Max?" Brian asked, pointedly looking at Thomas, who focused his concentration on buttering a piece of bread.

"Of course," she said. "Max isn't serious. We have fun and flirt a little but that's the extent of our relationship. See, as long as you don't get caught up, it's harmless. It's only when you believe in fantasy that you get into trouble."

"Well, that's a relief," said Rob. "For a moment I thought you were one of those people who dress up in elf costumes and get married on YouTube.

Everyone laughed until Brian said in a louder than necessary voice. "I guess the real question is does Max know you have a boyfriend?"

She ignored his question and it took every ounce of nerve for Thomas to stop shaking and compose himself enough to stand up.

No one really noticed, as Ron started telling a racy story about a blind date with a woman who kept asking him question after question as if he were on an interview "She was beautiful, but man, she was all business. I think her face would have turned to stone and crumbled if she'd smiled."

In as even a voice as he could muster, Thomas excused himself, telling Brian he'd wait for him in the car. His soon-to-be-ex-associate merely nodded, not even glancing at him. Thomas, on the verge of another asthma attack, thought that they would stop him and beg him to stay, but no one said a word. Why would they? They were having too much fun. Instead, they let him go and sit in the cold.

From the car park, he could see her clearly. Could see her and Brian standing close together. Closer than was appropriate for two co-workers. Thomas watched as Brian placed a hand on her lower back. She let him. She didn't stop him as he moved in closer, his hand almost on her ass, whispering something in her ear that made her throw her head back with laughter.

His online girlfriend had turned out to be the flighty type. Worse of all, she didn't even care enough to tell people the truth about their flirtation. Strike that. They had a relationship. Was she forgetting all those late nights when they chatted intimately about everything? Thomas/Max told her things he'd never told anyone. Not that it mattered. In one fell swoop she had both cheated on him and relegated him to nothing status.

Thomas craned his neck to see what was happening and saw her standing in front of the window. Their eyes met for a few seconds. He sent her urgent telepathic messages. *Please recognize me. I'm Max. Can't you see?*

Thomas raised his hand in salutation, realizing with a pang that he resembled the little silver astronaut key ring in his pocket. He put his hand down quickly, but it didn't matter. She turned away, pretending she hadn't seen him.

It started to snow, the fat flakes covering the windshield. From a circle the size of a quarter, Thomas watched as the people from his work celebrated inside, warm and happy, eating and drinking, not giving a damn that the Space Cowboy sat alone, trembling in the car.

To: loveguru@ultimateguidetolove.com
Subject: Dear Love Guru

I recently met a guy online. He was funny and smart and we liked a lot of the same music. After we exchanged photos, I agreed to meet him at a café, you know, the way you suggested in your entry on meeting safely?

I was really nervous. We'd talked a few times on the phone, so conversation wasn't a problem. He was very good looking, in case you are wondering, he looked just like his photos, but in person he was so uncomfortable, so totally uptight. He kept staring at his watch. I wanted to ask him if he had another date lined up. It was off-putting. He was sweating too. Making small talk was painful, like having a tooth extracted. That's not a cliché, either. Before I had my braces fitted, they had to extract four molars and I swear it didn't hurt as much as meeting my date.

We decided to forgo dinner and went to the movies instead. Really, I should have dumped him there and then, but I thought sitting in the dark would be more like how it was online. You know, relax him or something? It didn't. Halfway through the film, he starts making these really weird breathing noises like Darth Vader puking up a hairball.

People were shouting at him to shut up. But his breathing got louder and more desperate. HRHFF. HRFHH. Think Dennis Hopper in *Blue Velvet*. He kept touching me too. Not my breasts, but putting his hand on my neck and shoulder.

I shrugged him off. I made it clear I wasn't interested. Oh my God, I was so embarrassed, I wanted to run out of the cinema but I was too scared. I went to the bathroom and stayed there for as long as I could, wondering if I should ditch him without saying anything.

It was only later, when I was in the lobby and saw the paramedics carrying him out that I understood. The entire time I'd been sitting there ignoring him, he was having an asthma attack. Someone called 911 while I was in the bathroom. He glared at me through his respirator.

Thing is, even if it is kind of my fault, he still owes me a reply. I've apologised a hundred times. I've explained, but he won't answer my emails. I mean, I thought we had something special. Now he doesn't want to talk to me. I hope you can post my letter, in case anyone runs into similar problems.

Signed,
Guilty.

ICICLES

CANDIDATE NUMBER 57 was gorgeous. Not cute in a good light, depends-on-your-tastes, kind of way. He was jaw-droppingly beautiful. Nina Parks didn't usually go for the chiselled, cheek-boned, Gaston from *Beauty and the Beast* type but she was drawn to his assurance and the confident way he moved, manoeuvring those Adonis-cum-Calvin-Klein limbs of his with unconscious grace. Here, finally, was a man who understood the power of his own body.

Nina immediately decided to shake up that confidence.

"It's good to finally meet you," he said, unwrapping his scarf and planting a light kiss on her cheek. He smelled sharp and clean like grapefruits. "You look beautiful."

If this had been a normal date and not part of Nina's 365-Date challenge, the evening might have gone differently. She reminded herself that this was strictly business. "Sorry," she said. "Do I know you?"

A smile broke out on his face. "Yes, in a way. I'm your date. At least I think I am." He pulled a sheet of paper from his pocket. "Bluesky. Wednesday. Seven sharp."

Nina took a sip of her drink.

"I'm pretty sure I'm in the right place. I even printed out your email. See? Oh wait," his smile faded. "Is this of those blind dating faux pas I'm always hearing about? Please tell me you're my date."

"Are you sure that's not your date over there?" Nina said, nodding across the room at a woman seated alone at a table with a tattered paperback.

"She doesn't look as if she's waiting for anyone. Although my date did say she liked reading."

"She is by herself," Nina added helpfully.

"So are you," he pointed out.

"Yes, but I'm enjoying my solitude. At least I was."

Candidate 57 knotted his eyebrows. For a split second, he let slip that silky confidence. Nina allowed herself a moment of pity for her date. Sure, he was good looking but he wasn't the brightest of men. First of all, the woman he was staring at was wearing a nondescript cardigan. No one looking to get lucky would ever dress like that on a date. Also, she was so engrossed in her book she never once looked at the handsome man who kept checking her out.

Candidate 57 sat down beside Nina, his long legs pressing next to hers under the tiny table.

"You're still here," she said. "I thought we established that your date was over there?"

"Perhaps," he said. "But I like it here."

Nothing about Candidate 57's online behaviour gave her any indication he'd be so bold. Nina's pre-date notes on him were concise and to the point: sweet, eager, good sport. Words that described the majority of the men she met on her challenges, although in person they rarely matched up to their online personas. Her current date, on the other hand, surpassed expectations. Nina wondered how it was possible that after all those hours of research and interviews; she still wasn't able to correctly pick out a decent man from the rubble when it counted. She made a mental note to be more probing in the future.

You are not planning on standing her up, are you?" Nina asked.

Candidate 57 glanced over at the other table. "I know I'm not supposed to say this, but when I saw you, it was immediately clear. *You* are the one I'm supposed to meet." He looked at Nina shyly, his long lashes casting a shadow against his cheeks in a way that made her have a split-screen moment where she was both outraged by his callousness toward his fake-blind-date, and grateful that despite the joke, he was exactly where he was supposed to be.

"You can't blame me for staying with you, can you?" he said. "It's destiny."

Nina ignored the gnawing sensation in her stomach. Most people would have recognized the sensation as regret, but Nina didn't do regret. She didn't do guilt either. She put the discomfort down to indigestion and ordered another drink.

"This is an unusual scenario," Candidate 57 said. "Most of the time I'm able to pick out the girl I'm supposed to meet, even in a room full of strangers."

"Next time ask for photos."

"I usually do, but my real date wasn't into that. To be honest, it was one of the things that most intrigued me."

"Not enough, or you'd be over there right now," Nina said.

"Touché," he said. "You know, I don't usually ditch my dates for beautiful, mysterious women sitting by themselves at a bar.

Nina gave him an inscrutable look.

"Honestly," said 57. "I've never purposely stood up anyone."

"I'm flattered," she said. "But you don't look like the type of guy who is into blind dates."

"Oh, I am. I guess my nerdiness isn't outwardly apparent, but I assure you. I'm as geeky as they come. You know, you should try virtual sometime. The people I've met online have been pretty decent. No connections but at the same time no disasters, which is a far cry from trying to meet someone in this city."

"Let's try now," Nina said. "Stand over there and text me on your mobile phone."

"That's not really the same thing."

"Humour me."

"Only if you promise to go out with me. Properly this time. Let me buy you dinner. Take you bowling, whatever it is you like to do."

"Maybe," said Nina, even though she had no intention of any such thing. Getting involved was an impossibility. She had 300 men left to date. Not to mention her contract, which prohibited her from seeing anyone outside the project. Even if the remainder of her candidates turned out to be mind numbing, socially dysfunctional fuckwads, she couldn't see Candidate 57 again.

"This is crazy," he texted, after he'd moved to another table.

57: Twitching badly. Can't type.

NP: Too much caffeine?"

57: Just nervous.

NP: Why? Bookworm guilt?

57: No. You. You make me nervous.

NP: No need to be. I don't bite. Unless you want me to. Oh wait. I forgot you're virtual.

Nina looked over and saw Rob the bartender, wiping glasses and pretending he wasn't watching them.

NP: You still there?

57: Scratch what I said about virtual. Prefer to be with you.

NP: You sure? It's not too late to show up to your real date.

57: Made my choice. Destiny. Remember?

NP: You know what? I'm going for a walk. Want to come?

57: But it's freezing out there.

NP: OK then, stay here all night and txt me.

57: I'll get my coat.

As they walked to the door, they paused in front of the woman with the mousy hair who was still reading.

"That's some book," said Nina. "You think she knows you've ditched her?"

"If zombies invaded the Bluesky she wouldn't notice," said Candidate 57, as he guided her out of the Bluesky.

"I can't believe you suggested this. It's freezing," he said. "Why aren't we inside, sipping something warm in front of the fireplace?"

"Because then you would miss this fabulous view. Nina pointed to the skyscrapers surrounding the lake like sentient soldiers. "Don't they look like they're protecting the city? When I first moved here, I would spend hours on this park bench, watching the lights shooting steel and glass into the sky."

"It's perfect," he said. "So incredibly perfect."

"You aren't appreciating the view."

"Trust me, I am," he said.

"Come on, let's go ice skating." Nina said, leading them to a frozen pond.

"Isn't that dangerous?" Candidate 57 asked, testing the edge of the ice with his boot. "Aren't you afraid of falling through?"

"Don't worry, she laughed. "It's frozen over." Nina launched herself onto the ice and performed a pirouette. In her shoes she skated the perimeter of the pond, stopping in front of him. "Try it," she said.

He took her hand and they twirled around together, looking like figure skaters in a snow globe.

Afterward, Nina couldn't recall what they talked about. Their dialogue relied less on words than on body language—on murmurs, assents and synchronicity. She had forgotten how intoxicating that kind of shorthand could be.

It wasn't until the wet flakes touched her cheeks that she realized it was snowing. The flakes were clinging to the rooftops of buildings and houses like powdered sugar, making the entire city look like a giant gingerbread house.

"You know, online or off, most first dates are awkward, surreal affairs," Candidate 57 said. "I've never been out with someone and felt that silent click, that immediacy I'm feeling right now." His voice faltered slightly, as if he were uncomfortable discussing metaphysical vagaries. "So much is lost in misunderstandings. You spend an enormous amount of time clarifying what you really mean."

"So why persist?"

"Because I'm an optimist." He wiped a snowflake from her cheek.

"I think it is time to go home now," Nina said. "Thank you for the company."

"You're leaving? I thought we were having a good time."

"We are, but I really must go." She stood up.

"Wait," he said, pulling gently on her sleeve. "I want to tell you something. You know earlier, when I said my date was unusual? I wasn't referring to the woman with the book."

Nina raised an eyebrow.

"I've known all along that you were my real date. I recognized you immediately. Even with you trying to trick me, I knew it was you. Please don't ask how. I've been trying to figure it out all night."

"Why didn't you say something sooner?"

"I was going along with it. For some reason you wanted me to believe otherwise. But let me tell you something, if that other woman had been my *real* date I would never have gone off with you, no matter how cute you were, sitting there sipping your drink. I'm just not that kind of guy. So if you want to leave because I failed some sort of test, please reconsider. I think there is something between us," he said, looking directly at her. "And if you feel the same way, I'd like to see you again."

Nina felt the pang from earlier spread from her stomach to her ribs. A part of her wished she could be honest with him. "I'm a writer," she would say. A writer with a blog on how to seduce men online." Most likely he would not look kindly on her after that. But then he had gone along with the lie about the other woman. Perhaps she was underestimating him.

Stop it Nina, she told herself. Stop fumbling and cut it off cleanly. Don't be tempted to feel pity for yourself or for him. It's an amateur move that will derail all those months of hard work. Stop being bubble-headed. You need to focus.

"I take it by your silence that your answer is no." He released her arm.

"It's complicated. I can't explain. But before I leave, I need to ask you something."

"Sure," he said.

"What about me did you like? Online, I mean."

"*Everything.*"

"Come on," said Nina.

"I'm serious. You're smart, confident. Self-assured. When I'm talking to you I feel excited and at the same time, calm, despite the obvious nerves. With you I'm allowed to be myself."

"I find that hard to believe."

He gave her a sad little smile. "If you want to know the truth, that's what I most like about you. You talk a good game but we're alike in many ways. And at the same time we're unique, like snowflakes, each of us hopelessly convinced that some day we'll find our perfect match. Thing is, how can you see your way in all that blinding swirl?"

"I'm not much of a snowflake girl," she said. "I prefer icicles. There's no misunderstanding icicles. They're not looking for anything. They have their moment to shine and then they fade away."

"I never thought about it that way," he said. "But you're right. They have a certain beauty."

"I'd like to go home now."

"OK," he said. "But first you have to answer my question. Why don't you want to see me again? Is there someone else?"

"No, nothing like that."

"What is it?"

Nina shook her head.

"You poor thing. You're shivering," he said. They stopped under a streetlight and Candidate 57 unravelled his scarf and placed it around her neck. He kissed her gently on her exposed throat, wrapping her up in the soft cashmere until everything except her eyes was covered. "You need to dress more warmly," he scolded. "Otherwise you'll get sick."

Nina wanted to tell him that she never got sick. She was seldom afraid or anxious or nervous like other people. He was wrong about them being similar. She knew the truth about snowflakes. She let go of his hand as they made their way out of the park.

Nina Parks lay in bed unable to sleep. Outside, the city was covered in snow, muffling the sound of cars and taxis. The absence of noise made her feel disoriented. She kept waking up, wondering where she was.

For a moment, she almost allowed herself to forget her challenge. Being with Candidate 57 was both hypnotically reassuring and electric, like sitting too close to a fireplace. She was aware that the feeling had little to do with her or him. Half the time, she wasn't even aware of the words coming out of his mouth. It was like automatic writing, but with their libidos.

After all that time spent in virtual environments. All those years of spreadsheets, interviews, advice, and finally, an honest to goodness, real connection—as strong physically as it was virtually—and she wasn't able to take it anywhere. Candidate 57 had to remain behind as an entry—an anecdote about a frozen lake. Tomorrow, when Nina didn't answer his emails, and later, his desperate texts, he'd understand that the connection he had so valiantly pursued was one-sided.

"My objectivity has been temporarily eclipsed by a wave of single-minded lust," Nina wrote. "Blindsided by desire, I am unable to get over the physicality of him, even while understanding the demands of my desperate body. I am usually detached when I need to be. It's embarrassing to admit that despite my focus, I have turned out to be a pulsing, mutating organism with urges, just like anyone else. I am not the unbiased observer of human nature I thought I was. Who am I to preach about discipline and clear-headed choices, when my own body waits to betray me at every turn?"

"Good morning, beautiful," Candidate 57 said, standing near the window and wrapping his arms around her. "What are you writing?"

"Nothing," said Nina, closing her notebook.

Together, they watched the morning bathe the sky in fingers of white and gold. The sun came out, making the gingerbread city grey with sludge. After everything had melted, and they had seen the icicles turn to broken glass and then to nothing, Candidate 57 took Nina by the hand and led her back to bed.

DON'T EAT THE PRAWN

CLAUDE, A 33-YEAR-OLD British businessman, was the first to respond to Charlotte's ad in Match Made in Heaven. His profile listed an eclectic collection of hobbies ranging from poetry to Puccini. He was into sailing, Japanese cookery and French films.

Describing himself in twenty words or less, Claude wrote: *I am an incurable romantic, a passionate humanitarian—a bon vivant who knows how to enjoy life.* Under 'What actor or celebrity do you most resemble?' he replied: *Young Harrison Ford.* His photo showed a tanned handsome man, wearing a navy polo and jeans. Han Solo, posing as sea captain.

They flirted on the dating website for six days before agreeing to meet for dinner in the Rum Rum Drum, a French restaurant in the city.

"Charlie, right?" Claude said, kissing Charlotte on both cheeks. "So sorry. The cab driver couldn't find the place. I recognized you immediately, even from across the room. Sometimes you don't know what you get on these matchmaking sites, but you are *Va Va Voom. Très mignone.*" He put his fingertips to his mouth and made a lip-smacking sound. "You're much more attractive than your photograph."

Unfortunately, Charlotte couldn't say the same for Claude. Despite the interesting accent, her date was stout, bald, and looked closer to 43 than 33. He wore pressed linen trousers and boat shoes with no socks. He looked nothing at all like Harrison Ford, young or old.

He laughed and patted his belly, as if he could read her mind. "Yes, well you know what they say, the camera puts on ten pounds."

And subtracts height and hair, thought Charlotte.

"Would you like some champagne? It's the least I can do for making you wait."

On her profile she had written that champagne was her favourite drink, even though she'd only had it twice in her life: once at her wedding, and once at a department store event where they were promoting stem-ware.

Claude called the waitress over and ordered a bottle of Veuve Clicquot. When the bottle arrived, he filled her glass to the top and proposed a toast.

"*Salut,*" he said.

"*A votre sante,*" said Charlotte.

"Are you Catholic?"

"I was referring to the toast."

"I don't get it. Anyway, what do you think?"

"Delicious."

"About the place I mean. Great find, huh?"

The Rum Rum Drum was decorated in early bordello meets *Dante's Inferno* and was packed with businessmen and platinum-haired girls wearing their lingerie to dinner.

"The service is flawless. And the food is unbelievable. *C'est magnifique.*" Claude kissed his fingers again. "You must try everything. Please tell me you are not one of those salad pecking types."

Charlotte shook her head.

"I didn't think so," he said, eyeing Charlotte up and down. "You're much too curvy. Me, I'm a bit of a foodie." He ordered a dozen oysters to start and broiled lobster with extra butter for his main course. Seafood, he informed his date, was his favourite aphrodisiac.

"You're smiling now. That's better, Charlie. Loosen up and live life to the full. Otherwise it just passes you by."

"You're right."

"Of course I am. Why do people feel the need to behave all the time? Where is the fun in that?" He grinned like a naughty schoolboy and refilled their glasses.

Charlotte sat back in the booth letting the bubbles tickle her tongue.

"How long did you say you'd been with Match Made in Heaven," asked Claude.

"Just a week before I met you."

"Is that so? So I'm your first?"

The way he said it made Charlotte flush. "And you?"

"Six weeks. I'm so tied up with work that I find it hard to meet people. So far, the dates haven't really met my expectations. They're nice girls, don't get me wrong, they're just not my cup of tea. Although, I must say I lucked out tonight." He looked her up and down appreciatively and she felt herself blush again. It had been a while since a man had made her feel tingly inside. He pressed his thigh against hers, as he leaned in to give her an oyster. She didn't move away.

To think she'd almost said no to meeting him. Charlotte enjoyed reading his emails and the buzz of anticipation before opening each one, but she didn't want a relationship. She was married to Tom, a decent, hard-working man who had lost interest in her less than a year into their marriage. Claude showered her with the attention she longed for. And anyway, online dating wasn't the same as going out to a bar to pick up a man.

When the food came, it was just as delicious as Claude said. They alternated between feeding each other little morsels and cooing over how scrumptious everything was. When it was Claude's turn to feed her, he kept 'accidentally' brushing against her bare arms and shoulders, so that she was breathless by the time the food reached her mouth. She closed her eyes and tasted the rich seafood, the creaminess of the shrimp with crabmeat and truffle sauce, and the lightness of the pink champagne. So this was what it was like to be seduced.

"Now, now, Charlie," said Claude, placing his hand on top of hers. "You might want to slow down a little. You don't want it to go to your head."

She opened her eyes as the waitress set down two glasses of whisky.

"I thought we'd break up the monotony and try something with a little edge. Go on, taste it."

Charlotte picked up her glass and swallowed an inch of the amber liquid before sputtering it out over the table.

"Careful now, that's not water. That's reserve scotch."

"I'm sorry. I wasn't expecting it to burn."

The waitress gave Charlotte a little smile. "Can I get you anything else?"

"I can think of a few things," Claude said. He craned his neck to watch her backside as she slinked away. "My, my. She reminds me of a burnished hunter Goddess. You know, that six-foot regal one? What's her name?" He snapped his fingers.

"Athena? Diana? Artemis?"

"No. No."

"Greek, Roman or Celtic?"

"On the telly. You know, from New Zealand? Big tits, dark hair."

"Xena, Warrior Princess?"

"That's the one." He let out a low wolf whistle and held his hands in front of his chest. "Body like a brick shithouse. I wouldn't kick her out of bed for eating crackers."

Charlotte was so startled she dropped her napkin. Whatever bad things could be said about the décor of the Rum Rum Drum, its carpets could not be faulted. Luxurious and plush, she could have spent the evening curled up on the floor.

The effects of all those drinks were starting to catch up to her. Was Claude joking about the waitress? He had to be. Who said things like that? It must be that weird British sense of humour. Over email, Claude had sounded refined and exotic, but his guttural accent was beginning to grate.

"Charlie, did you hear me? What on earth are you doing down there? You're not jealous are you?"

"What?" she said, plopping herself back on her seat. "Of course not. Don't be silly."

"Are you sure? I know how you women get. You act open-minded at first and then turn into possessive cows."

"Cows? Well, I'm not like that. You don't have to worry about me."

"Good. Because you have your own charms, you know. You have nothing to be embarrassed about. You have adequate tits and good legs for a woman your age. You should feel proud." He reached out and squeezed her shoulder. "Come on drink up. We have another one coming."

Charlotte took a tentative sip and although she didn't spit it out this time, she still felt like gagging as it made its way down her throat.

"HA HA," Claude laughed. "Outrageous. Please tell me you don't make that face in bed. I didn't peg you as having a sense of humour. It's usually only the ugly ones that have good personalities."

Claude finished his scotch and let out a belch. He leaned against the leather of the booth, undid his belt and slipped off his shoes, releasing his sweaty, hairy feet from their unjust imprisonment.

"So, Charlie, you're 31 *and* single. How's that possible? Why hasn't someone snapped you up already? You should have a man in your life. Going that long without regular sex isn't healthy."

I do have a man and it's been a while since I was 31, she thought. "The past is the past. I'm ready to meet someone new."

"Ta-da. Today's your lucky day." He placed his hand on her knee. "Come a little closer. I want to show you this." Claude slid a gold key in her direction. It was shaped in the form of a perverted bunny with an overbite.

"What's that?"

"This place is an exclusive club. One of my clients is a member. He lets me use his key from time to time. I've reserved a room for us upstairs."

His eager, damp hand slid past her knee to her thigh.

Charlotte looked around the Rum Rum Drum. It made sense now. The businessmen, the expensive red leather, the half dressed women. Her stomach lurched.

"Are you alright? I hope it's not the food," said Claude. "I was ill from food poisoning once. I spent days with it coming out from both ends. I make it a policy to never to order prawns. Did you get that, Charlie? Never order the prawn. Bloody common sense. If I were you, I'd go to the toilet and try to have a little, you know *dump*. It will make you feel right as rain.

"I think I'm going to go home."

Claude frowned, his small eyes pinched together so closely, they looked as if they were going to touch. "But we haven't had pudding yet."

"Maybe another time."

"I've already paid for the room."

"Excuse me?"

"I paid for the room," he said, through clenched teeth. "Charlotte, I thought we had an *understanding*. I thought we both wanted the same thing. Look, I'm quite fatigued and you look like you could use some freshening up. Let's play it by ear. See what happens."

The thought of going home to make herself a mug of herbal tea was wrangling with her image of the strong, independent woman out on an adventure. Charlotte was always choosing the safe option and now here she was again, wanting to run away before anything exciting happened. She'd gone through all the trouble. Claude wanted her. Why not throw caution to the wind?

"Why not?" she whispered.

"What's that," Claude asked.

"I said, what are we waiting for?"

"That's the spirit," he said, cheering up considerably. "You wait and see. We're going to have a grand evening." Claude led his date up the stairs, one hand firmly on her back.

The room was furnished in much the same way as the restaurant: red walls and throw pillows. The bed was enormous, almost as wide as the room itself. Claude dove headlong into it.

"Join me," he said to Charlotte, patting the bed.

"I have to freshen up. Why don't you order us some more champagne?"

"Good idea," he said, reaching for the phone.

In the bathroom, she washed her face with cool water, wishing she didn't feel so queasy. She was not used to being wined and dined. Even after she married, Tom had never been one for excess. Twice a month, he would shut-off his computer after dinner, close all the curtains in the house, until no sliver of light remained, and lay on the bed in his boxers and black socks. Charlotte, taking her cue, would join him in her cotton nightgown. They'd embrace for exactly one minute. Then Tom would remove his underpants, mount her and perform his marital duties for a further two and a half minutes, before rolling off and going to sleep.

Claude reeked of whisky and he was nowhere near Charlotte's romantic ideal, but it was better than being with a husband who was never impulsive, who never lost control, who was punctual, even when having sex.

Charlotte had told only one person that she was registered on Match Made in Heaven. She thought her sister would understand.

"If you are unhappy that's one thing, but meeting men while you're still married isn't right," Rachel said.

"I thought you couldn't stand Tom."

"I can't. But it's not right to go behind his back like that."

"It's not *cheating* if I don't plan on having sex. It's just a little fun. A little flirting. You don't get it. You have a love life. You have a husband who adores you. Tom has dinner at 7:00, news at 8:00, and bed by 9:00. You know what he's like."

"That's not reason enough to resort to creeps."

"Rachel, they're not all like that. Some of them are lonely and sweet."

"Jesus, Charlie, those websites attract bottom feeders. Don't you get it? It's not even dating. It's paid sex. You think they're being *sweet*, but those guys are only looking to get laid. They responded to you because you're naïve and gullible. Why else would anyone go looking for love online?"

"Because my husband is boring. What do you want from me?" Charlotte said, putting the phone down on her sister.

So what if she was a little gullible? Wasn't everyone when it counted? She rinsed her mouth, applied perfume, combed her hair and burst into tears. She couldn't go through with it.

She couldn't go out there and have sex with a virtual stranger. She'd have to come clean, tell Claude she was married. Except she couldn't do that either. Her unhappy relationship wasn't anyone business. Charlotte had a feeling that it wouldn't make much of a difference to her date anyway. He would just say that they were consenting adults and hey, why the hell not, since they were both there?

She wished she had never tried eDating. The blog she'd read about empowering your love life made it sound easy. You signed up. You posted an attractive photo, men emailed and you selected the one you were interested in. *Voila*. Instant romance.

"Are you alright in there?" Claude called out. "You haven't fallen asleep on me, have you?"

She dabbed at her face with a towel and tried to imagine what Nina Parks, the author of the article would do if she were in a similar situation. She sounded edgy and bold, the kind of person who would waltz right in and take matters in her own hands instead of waiting for romance to fall into her lap. Unlike Charlotte, she wouldn't have waited 38 years to have her first love affair. She wouldn't have rushed into a bad marriage, believing she had no other options. She certainly wouldn't be crying on a cold porcelain tub when she could be out there with her date drinking bubbly.

Charlotte was tired of settling for whatever life threw her way. This was her chance to gain control, to stop blaming others for her unhappiness. If there were regrets, she'd worry about them later, on the way home. Now was the time to act. She carefully stepped out of her dress, removed her panties and walked out of the bathroom.

ORANGES

Mica, my online boyfriend, trusted only the things he could see and touch. To him the words of the body were like gospel.

"But people lie in person," I said to him over chat one evening. "They lie ruthlessly to your face. They are dishonest while lying underneath you in bed. Our hearts lie, our hands lie. Our fingers itch to tell untruths."

"And your mind, Lyra? Is your mind free of guile?"

I responded that truth and lies don't exist as abstract concepts. In order to deceive, you first needed a body.

"That's such metaphysical bull. Repeat after me, Lyra: I am not a concept. I am a person. You can't disconnect from your body whenever it's convenient."

We were chatting past midnight, our usual time. I was staring at the camera positioned on top of my computer screen. Not that I had ever used it with Mica. In the past, with other men, I was the one desperate to see and touch—the one who insisted on meeting so I could show off my assets face-to-face.

Mica accused me of having problems with physicality. He liked imagining me as a recluse he was reprogramming back into society.

Mica: The problem is that you live in a fantasy world.

Lyra: And where do you live?"

Mica: In reality, of course.

Mica liked to draw lines in hypothetical sand. At the start of our relationship, we took roles on opposite sides of the virtual-versus-reality divide. Now it was too late to change, even if I resented the larger-than-life V he had pinned to my chest.

Mica: Lyra the rebel. The free thinker. The one gazing at an infinite sky while the rest of us make-do with a box.

Lyra: So free yourself. You are more than what you can see and touch. Your mind creates its own reality, even if it interprets things in ways you don't necessarily agree with.

Mica: I find it hard to talk to you when you are like this.

Lyra: Why don't you just admit that maybe I'm right? It isn't necessary to be together to be *together*.

Mica: Has anyone ever told you how much you sound like Yoda?

Lyra: Better Yoda than a die-hard pessimist.

Mica: *Realist.* And I'm afraid that until we meet, you will remain as abstract as your explanations.

Lyra: That's ridiculous. I am not something you've conjured out of a handful of dirt and imagination. Don't you get it, Mica? I'm as real as it gets.

Mica: Maybe you are, but this is not real. Otherwise, we wouldn't be having this discussion.

Lyra: What would we be doing?

Mica: Kissing, for starters. Kissing and forgetting this whole tired argument.

Lyra: You think a kiss is going to make us forget everything?

Mica: By your reply I can only assume you've never been kissed properly. If you were here now, I guarantee you wouldn't be able to utter a single rebuttal. My tongue would be so firmly lodged in your mouth, you wouldn't be able to.

Team Reality scores two points.

Despite Mica's need to shut me up, I'm too busy swooning to come up with a decent reply. "So kiss me," I finally say.

Mica: Kissing online is a poor substitute.

Lyra: Not if you do it properly.

Mica: Properly, how, Ly?

Lyra: Close your eyes and I'll show you.

Mica: You know, that's one of the things I hate about all this virtual stuff. I never know if you are being serious. Are you serious?

"Of course," I say, happy that he can't see my lack of conviction. Nonetheless, somewhere deep inside I believe what I'm saying. Otherwise, why would I persist? "Go on," I say again. "Close your eyes."

Mica: How do I know you aren't doing your nails or watching television? You could be preparing your taxes while pretending to be into me. How would I know?

Lyra: Trust me. I mean every word.

Mica: Tell me what you are actually doing. Right now.

Lyra: Right this minute?

Mica: Yeah.

Lyra: I'm eating dinner.

Mica: I rest my case.

Lyra: Wait, that's not fair. I didn't get a chance to earlier. I rushed here from work. I was so eager to talk to you. It has nothing to do with pretending. You can kiss me now. I've finished.

Mica: Forget it.

Lyra. Come on, Mica. Kiss me.

Mica: No.

Lyra: Pucker your lips.

Mica: Stop it. I don't want to play this game anymore.

My online boyfriend was easily the most literal person I'd ever met. Linear. Logical—a straight-flying arrow spouting facts and figures. Yet despite his limitations, I was deeply attracted to him—perhaps because he so badly wanted to pull me to *terra firma*.

The other night we tried cybersex.

"This is creepy," Mica said. "I feel as if I'm in a Woody Allen film. The one where the couple orgasms without touching."

Lyra: *Sleeper?*

Mica: That's the one.

Lyra: I love that film.

Mica: Why am I not surprised?

Lyra: What's that supposed to mean?

Mica: Sex is not supposed to be clinical.

Lyra: You think I like it that way?

Mica: I don't know how you like it. I'd like to find out. As long as we do it properly, face-to-face, not online.

Lyra: I don't think desire can be contained in one neat scenario. What about peep shows? What about prisoners and conjugal visits? Think about it.

Mica: I'd rather not.

Lyra: The whole touching-through-a-screen thing can be an interesting experience if you're into that kind of thing.

Mica: Well I'm not.

Lyra: Relax. You've fantasized about women before, right?

Mica: What does that have to do with anything?

Lyra: Cybersex is like that, but better because it's not one-sided. It's a case of imagination and reality coming together in real time.

Mica: In my fantasies, you and I don't have metaphysical conversations in the middle of sex.

Lyra: Imagine if we did though? We'd be going all hot and heavy, until one of us shouts out Descartes' name.

Mica: Oh God. Talking is making it worse. Can we stop now?

I asked myself for the hundredth time why Mica was so threatened by virtuality. Why didn't he understand that this was how some people chose to live their lives?

"You know what I would like to do?"

"No," I say. "Tell me."

"I want to drag you into the light, Lyra. Kicking and screaming if I have to, so we can settle this in person. The whole virtual thing is a sham. We are meant to live among other people. Not hidden away behind our screens."

Is that how he saw me? Like some socially disfigured geek creeping around in the darkness, Phantom of the Opera style? *Quelle horreur*.

"You're a princess. A virtual princess stuck in her pretend tower," he says.

I tell him that I'm not the type to sit around wringing my hands, wondering what's taking him so long to save me. Lucky for him, I'm a 21st century girl who doesn't need saving. Least of all by some virtually-challenged doubting Thomas.

Mica: I'm not so sure.

Lyra: Mica, if you have an orange and give me half, how many oranges do you have?

Terminal Romance

Mica: Not the orange conversation again.

Lyra: Yes the orange conversation. You don't seem to understand it any other way.

Mica: You have only one orange. You've already told me this story.

Lyra: One orange. Two halves. The difference is one of timing. Before you cut it, there was one orange living in its totality on the counter in the kitchen. With its two sides now on a plate, it is still ONE orange. Two sides of the same fruit. Not two distinct oranges. So which one is the real slice? Neither. It's an invalid question, as they are both part of the same thing.

Team Virtuality scores 2 points.

"Look, I don't really care about oranges," Mica says. "When I'm hungry, I peel one and put it in my mouth. Its purpose is to be eaten. Not to be an instruction on the duality of mind and body. We exist to be physical. I cannot accept you as real without tasting you first."

"So that's it? You want to take me out for a test spin before you figure out what you want?" I laugh out loud and realize with a pang that I have never heard the sound of Mica's laughter. I have no idea what it sounds like. Right now I'm not even sure if he is the type of person who knows how to laugh.

Mica: How can I believe anything is real between us when I can't see your face?

Lyra: You are here with me now. We're together. We're sharing this moment. I'm not a fantasy. I'm as real as you are.

Mica: Don't you see? I'm never going to be like you, Ly. I'm not content to live in my head. I need something tangible. Something to hold on to.

I need something tangible too but I don't say anything. I wish he would understand that what we share is more than most people get. Our connection is almost palpable. But *almost* is not good enough for Mica.

Mica: Let's stop talking and meet. You are always going on about how the body lies, but the body also tells the truth. Are you game?

Lyra: Are you saying all I have to do is show up to some impromptu date and you'll believe anything, even if I'm lying, because you can see me?

Mica: Yes. Except the point would be moot by then.

Lyra: Tell me, Mica. Tell me how you can tell the difference between truth and lies?

Mica: Years of experience. Body language. I don't know. I just can.

If Mica would only stop and listen to what I'm saying, things would be better between us. Relationships don't always work the way he thinks they do. I can't deny my feelings; they were instant and definite within ten minutes of meeting him. Maybe it will be the same way in person. But maybe not.

"There are no guarantees," I tell him.

"Words are no longer enough. I need to see you," he says. There it was again, Mica's ultimatum—at least once an evening and less and less veiled as time went on.

Mica: From your silence I gather you don't want to meet?

Lyra: That's not true. It's just that I've been out with men I've met online before. It's artificial. Meaningless—like reading a script written by someone else.

Mica: It wouldn't be that way with us. I wouldn't ruin it by saying anything trite. Even sitting in silence with you is better than our best conversation, don't you think?

Lyra: I happen to like our long intimate moments. Why rush things? I thought we were having fun.

Mica: Rush? It's been weeks. We should have met by now.

Lyra: Faith, Mica. You don't have any faith. You don't trust what's inside you. You doubt everything I say. You even doubt your own feelings.

Mica: Meet me and I'll believe everything.

Lyra: Why do you insist on conditions? That's not how faith works. You are dependent on the whole physicality thing.

Mica: Because I need to see what you look like before I decide how I feel? Because I want to hold you in my arms, instead of typing out long descriptions?

Lyra: You make too much out of touching and seeing. That's not what we're about.

Mica: Really? I thought that was exactly what we're about. You can't pry your mind and body apart like the two halves of your stupid metaphysical orange.

Mica didn't type anything for a while. I knew he was upset, but I wasn't going to budge. Even when I wanted him so badly, I ached. He made me feel as if I were having a one-way conversation with myself, as if I were in this alone, a sad-faced ghost, haunting the edges of the ether world. I wanted him to have a tiny bit of belief in us. Maybe then I would agree to meet him. But Mica wanted things his way or no way at all.

I tried another angle. "Look, we have something special. You know we do. You can't underestimate it, even if we can't see one another."

"Can't or won't?"

"It doesn't matter. We have a connection," I said, aware it sounded lame.

Mica: That's all you can come up with? I have to settle for some force field effect and forget I have needs and desires? You don't really get it. Do you, Lyra?

Lyra: I'm trying to but the *'I have needs'* excuse is pretty sad. How many women have you tried this with?

Mica: What with?

Lyra: *This.* An online relationship.

Mica: This is NOT a relationship. This is nothing. That's what I keep telling you. We started out with a bang but everything feels like we're pretending now. It doesn't keep me warm at night. I want more.

Lyra: It feels pretty real to me. I'm happy with what we have.

Mica: Of course you are—you believe your own hype. You know what? Pretending to walk the moon is not the same thing as actually experiencing it.

Lyra: Thank you, Neil Armstrong.

Mica: Lyra, this way of life may seem cute to you, but it's backward. Everything requires so much thought. Some things should be instant. I want to be able to reach out and feel you, not *talk* about feeling you.

Lyra: Reach out and touch faith.

Mica: What?

Lyra: Never mind. Look, don't over analyse things. Close your eyes and feel me.

Mica: No.

Lyra: Put one leg on either side of the hemisphere. Straddle the divide. There is only one world and it is a lot smaller than you imagine.

Mica: I'm sorry. I can't do this anymore.

Lyra: Fine. Let's talk about something else.

Mica: No, you don't understand. I don't want any of this. Not with you. Not like this.

Lyra: ?

Mica: You can't say I didn't give it a try. Look, I like you. Probably more than I should. But this is too weird. Do you know how it feels not be able to hold you whenever I want?

I can't touch you. I can't kiss you. I can't reassure you or make you happy.

Lyra: You do make me happy.

Mica: Wait. Let me finish. Am I supposed to be comforted by typing things back and forth? That's not a relationship, that's torture. Can't you see that?

Lyra: I wasn't aware you wanted me like that.

Mica: I wish things had been different. If you lived nearby, maybe we'd have a shot. Except, I don't even know where you live.

Lyra: Does it matter?

Mica: Jesus! Of course it matters. Do you want to be virtual forever? Is that it? You've never even considered getting together with me?

"Of course I have," I say, wanting to tell him that I was waiting for the right time. I don't, because I know he wouldn't understand. When you get physical right away it can be jolting, like rushing into a cold sea after being out in the sun all afternoon.

Mica: It's too late. I can't do this anymore.

I read his messages flashing on my screen and try not to panic, but the invisible cord that has held us together these past few weeks is frayed and easing up on my end. An unfair tug-of-war.

Team Reality scores two more points.

This whole thing is stupid. We should be on the same side. Whatever our views, we should forget our opposing ideologies and merge the way we were meant to from the first instant we felt that pull.

I tell myself to remain calm, wondering if I can say anything to make him stay. Maybe I can offer to turn on my webcam. That might buy me some time. But is there a point now? No matter how many times I explain about the oranges, Mica will never agree that we're not so very different.

I am, and will always be, a virtual girl to him, for better or worse. I'm destined to play my designated role to the end.

"Best of luck," says my former cyber boyfriend.

Mica: Maybe someday you'll find a man who will see things the way you do. I'm sorry it didn't work out.

Lyra: Wait. Mica…

Mica: Please don't say it. It won't do any good. I won't believe you anyway. Let's just leave it at that.

Mica logs off.

It hurt. I won't lie. It hurt like someone was ripping wires from my chest. Mica would have been happy to know that the pain was not just in my mind. It extended from my fingertips to ignite every nerve in my body. The pain was so intense, I lay curled on my bed, waiting for the spasms and nausea to subside.

Final score: Reality 6. Virtuality 2.

Mica had given me up. No. It was worse than that. He'd given *us* up. We had a connection, but he was unwilling to go with his instinct, choosing to tear us apart at the seams because he couldn't understand how I worked.

I wish I had been that physical presence he craved so much, if only so he could see the truth written on my face and body. I wondered if Mica had sabotaged all his other relationships in the same way. If he had stood there, resolute and stubborn, as he had with me, refusing to face what was so obvious, focusing instead on the meaningless details. Now I'll never know. I'll never know how a pessimistic-realist ever lets go enough to fall in love.

Instead of feeling sorry for myself, I stand up and wash my face. I make a pot of coffee, pop some aspirin and head back to my computer. One advantage of not being physical is how quickly I can get back on my feet.

"Hello," I say to the next linear man I meet. "I'm Jillian Jones, Virtual Girl. Would you like to play?"

THE ALL IMPORTANT FACE-TO-FACE

From The Ultimate Guide to Finding Love Online by Nina Parks

I'VE HAD EMAILS asking where I stand on the whole face-to-face issue. Since I wasn't aware this was a problem for my readers, let me say this. Do NOT get caught up in the 'What If' game.

WHAT IF we have something special that can't be measured or understood by other people and WHAT IF we make up our own rules and decide not to meet in person, because WHAT IF this virtual thing is more real than that other reality?

Don't be tempted to think this game is real. For one, it distracts you from the reality of your situation. And your situation is pretty clear. You are human. Not a cyborg. At some point you are going to have to meet to see if all that online whatiffing is real and not some elaborate wishing on your part.

Now when I say *real* I'm not referring to those off-line, superficial, sight-only constructs that non-virtual people are always going on about. Words and opinions hold more weight for me than physical attributes. But no matter how infatuated, I refuse to throw away common sense for the sake of a few well-written lines. What I am saying is that there is no singular reality. In other words, not meeting your online *inamorato* is as short-sighted as believing the only genuine way to find romance is at a bar/party/church or cafe.

Are you with me? Good. Until you see and talk with your date in person, you will only be getting half the picture. Maybe you feel that making the transition from virtual is too stressful, but trust me, it is a mistake to believe the perfect romance is one where you never see one another. Faceless communication is far from ideal so don't spend months thinking how great you are together when you have no idea if that's true in person.

In order to have a successful relationship, you have to know a person's mind AND body. And when I refer to the body, I'm not talking about great hair and cheekbones. I am referring to minute mannerisms: the entire emotional smorgasbord that can be gleaned only from being physically together. Like it or not, there is undeniable truth written all over your body—and on his. If you deny yourself the chance to really get to know one another, how can you pretend to be in love?

And let's not forget the frustrating, ever-growing urges that accompany a virtual relationship. You see, chatting doesn't satisfy the longing for physical intimacy. You daydream about his hair and fingers, lips and skin. Skin! What glorious, amazingly hereto unappreciated wonder of biology. The desire to smell, touch and taste becomes so powerful you think you'll go mad from desire. Loneliness, which wasn't a problem before, is achingly constant.

As soon as you disconnect from your lover, time and space become relevant. Your mind says one thing: your body (unaware it is in conflict) says another. Like Alice, you tumble down the rabbit hole but you cannot shrink enough to fit through that pixelated door. While you emote in characters, you are not composed of bytes. You are flesh. Immutable. Feet of clay. Deal with it and stop wasting time. Meet him. Now.

MASQUERADE

CANDIDATE NUMBER 166 was a smartly dressed man in his 40s with salt and pepper hair, a grey pin-striped suit and Italian made shoes.

"My goodness," he said, as he entered the bar. "I had no idea you'd be so—*wow*." He stood admiring Nina Parks, his eyes taking in the tight skirt, silk stockings and four-inch heels. He called over the bartender and ordered champagne. "To shoes," he said.

"May we love them forever," Nina said, clinking her glass.

They met in a Second Life club called Footlong.

"Shoe size?" asked Pradaqueen, the key master. Prada was seven feet tall with platinum hair and a mirrored dress like a disco ball.

"Five, but I often wish my feet were bigger."

"No you don't, sweetie. It's hard to find beautiful shoes when you're a size eleven. How do you feel about garters," Prada asked, consulting the guest list.

"I only wear them on special occasions, such as now. Otherwise, I go barefoot. I love the feel of wood rubbing against my soles."

"So what else are you into, you little minx," said Prada.

"Honey," said Nina. "I'm into everything."

"You may enter."

Nina, who had never in her life been into feet, her own or anyone else's, was amused to find that Footlong was full of virtual salons dedicated to shoes. There were rooms for sitting and parading, a spa where you could give and receive foot massages, and stores where you could actually buy shoes. Her avatar joined in on everything. Her favorite was the ballroom, which blared out '70s hits that the chatters boogied to in their own living rooms, while they simultaneously watched themselves on their screens.

Despite her indifference to feet, Nina got on like a pair of Manolos with the members of Footlong. She put it down to a combination of open-mindedness and what she liked to call the 'Masquerade' factor. The Internet provided the perfect ballroom mask—a place where people with normal jobs and anonymous faces could indulge in unconventional behaviour without repercussions. It didn't matter if you were into lingerie, motorbikes, or life-sized dolls. What mattered was that people's tastes came in shades other than black and white.

"Can I say how refreshing it is to have such an outgoing person in our ranks?" said a man known as LouBoutin.

"Stop blatantly hitting on her," said his friend. "Please feel free to ignore him," he said to Nina. "Talk to me. I'm nice."

LouBoutin: And everyone knows 'nice' always wins the girl.

Nina: Tell you what. Why don't you both flirt with me?"

LouBoutin: Ooh, like a threesome?

Candidate 166: Subtle, Lou. Very subtle.

Nina: Think of it as a double date with trouble in the middle.

LouBoutin: I'd love to, I really would, but I'm taken. My charming friend however is single. Single and in desperate need of female companionship.

Candidate 166: Great, make me look desperate.

LouBoutin: Desperate situations call for desperate measures.

Candidate 166: Stop. She'll think I'm incapable of speaking for myself.

LouBoutin: So speak. Tell her you want to have drinks with her and stop sending me private messages.

Nina: I know the perfect place to meet. They make the best martinis. I'm only sorry you can't make it as well, Lou.

LouBoutin: If I were single, I'd jump at the chance. But the old ball and chain would not be happy if I met up with you.

Nina: You're married?

LouBoutin: Ten years in October.

Nina: And does she know?

LouBoutin: About my *hobby*? Knows AND indulges.

Candidate 166: Some people have all the luck.

LouBoutin: Hey, your luck has just improved. You may be a discerning shoe lover, but you're a sorry state when it comes to women. Don't blow this. I want to hear all the dirty details.

***

"You know, I would never have guessed how urbane you were from the charade you and Lou had going online. Anyone would think you were romantically challenged," said Nina, as they sat in the Bluesky.

"Oh *that*. Lou finds it hilarious to serve me up as a lost cause."

"Really? I can't imagine you have problems meeting women."

"Meeting, no. It's keeping them that's the problem," said Candidate 166.

"So you lured me here under false pretences?"

"Is that why you said 'yes'? Because you felt sorry for me?"

"What can I say? I'm a sucker for a lost cause," said Nina.

"I'm starting to feel a bit like Quasimodo."

"Let me reassure you. You are definitely more Cary Grant than Quasi."

"Why thank you," said 166. "If I didn't know better, I'd blush. Now drink up, so I can buy you another."

This time when they toasted, his hand lightly brushed hers.

"So, tell me," Nina said. "How hard is it to find someone who shares your interests?"

"Nice way of putting it. It's easy to be accepting when everything is new and exciting, but girlfriends have a bad habit of wanting to change me. It comes down to ultimatums: outgrow your obsession or remain alone."

"Did you ever try to give it up for anyone?"

"Once or twice," he said, signalling the bartender for another drink. "It didn't work. You know that adage about old habits dying hard? I fell in love with shoes when I was four. My mother was a costume designer. She kept her favourite pairs on silk pillows. I spent my childhood literally in her closet, pretending I was Prince Charming. Why should I give up the very objects that have brought me such joy over the years?

From the Ultimate Guide to Finding Love Online

Rule one: Talk about things you are both interested in. Don't just rely on topics you have in common. Whatever you do, don't lie or pretend to be someone you are not.

"Are you always so unflinchingly honest?" Nina asked her date.

He nodded. "I tried hiding it at first but it's here to stay—my dirty little secret. Eventually people find out and then it's worse. Better to be open. Besides, I have nothing to be ashamed of. You'd think I was asking for the world instead of a little understanding."

"All because you're into shoes."

"Not just shoes. Stockings. Feet. Beautiful women wearing heels." He let a hand drop to caress Nina's ankle strap. "Those Choos fit you beautifully."

"Thank you. I bought them especially," she lied.

"You have great taste. I have a similar pair," he said, nodding at her feet with approval. "So, what about you, Nina? How do men react to your fetish?"

She stared at him blankly for a few seconds. "Oh, it's not really an issue. Women are supposed to be into shoes. That's a given. Plus, I can always convince someone to give me a foot massage. The whole foot fetish thing is more acceptable when you're female."

Candidate 166 laughed. "That's very true. Although sometimes it works in my favour to behave like a big dumb male."

He told Nina about his ongoing bet with Lou. On weekends, they'd go to the city to visit shoe stores, telling the salespeople they were looking for presents for girlfriends or wives. Then, acting confused over their options, they surreptitiously pocketed the little beige half-socks the store provided for their customers.

"I don't understand. Couldn't you just buy some panty hose and chop them up?"

"That would miss the point. They *have* to be worn, preferably recently, so they're still warm. The winner is the one who collects the most at the end of the year."

"So who is in the lead?"

"Do you have to ask?" he said, looking smug.

"How many footies do you have in total?"

"648."

Nina wolf-whistled. "What if there aren't any socks to be had?"

"Then we fall upon any shoes lying around." He described how he and Lou would dig their fingers into the leather, pretending to check the stitching, while feeling up the shape of the imprint left behind. "Extra points to whoever manages to get in a good long sniff."

"And no one has caught on?"

"We keep cultured pins on a map to track the stores we visit. We don't want them getting suspicious. Although sometimes I think Lou wants to get caught, just for the drama."

"I can't believe they don't notice," Nina said.

"If they do, they pretend not to. Can you imagine? They'd have our pictures taped at the back of stores like wanted criminals."

"*The Shoe Sniffing Bandits*," she laughed.

"Exactly."

"How about your personal collection? How many do you have?" she asked, sucking the olive from her martini.

"Come back to my place and I'll show you."

"Sly devil. And are they all designer?"

"I've been collecting for years. My last girlfriend complained they took up too

much space. She kept threatening to pack up my shoes and donate them to charity."

"Maybe she was secretly jealous."

"Maybe. When we first started dating, things were great between us. She had these amazing legs; ankles that made you want to cry. I bought her dozens of fabulous shoes. She preferred my stock, which I didn't like her wearing. 'They're for looking at, not for public consumption,' I'd say, only to come back from work to see her wearing my vintage Dior while vacuuming the apartment. In the end, she had to go."

"I'm sorry," Nina said, meaning it.

"Me too. I really liked her. I don't ask for much: a great sense of humour, beautiful, intelligent, a healthy respect for designer."

"That's not an impossible list."

Candidate 166 reached over and arranged a lock of Nina's hair that had fallen out of place. "That's because you're gloriously open-minded."

"Listen. I don't always. I mean, sometimes you can't believe."

"I understand, Nina. With me you don't have to explain or be ashamed. I'll never judge. That is, unless you wear cheap shoes. I won't stand for that."

She arched an eyebrow.

"I'm joking. A *little.*"

"See? Even you have your limits. The thing is no one can love anyone else unconditionally, no matter what they say. We aren't made that way."

"I guess you're right," said 166. "A friend of mine just got divorced because his wife could not, or would not, learn to play golf. Fourteen years of marriage, two children, and an inability to hit a decent drive splits them up."

"You're kidding."

"Golf was the excuse he gave, but I'm guessing he was tired of being misunderstood. The chasm opens up more and more until one day you wake up with nothing holding you together."

Rule two: If there is no spark, stay optimistic. People are an acquired taste. You may not like your date initially but with time you may grow to accept them.

They had moved from the bar to Candidate 166's car. Nina closed her eyes and leaned against the backseat. With the exception of the plush leather and the expensive bottle of champagne, it was like high school all over again.

Candidate 166 put on a classical CD and unfastened Nina's ankle straps. "How does that feel?" he said, stroking the arch of her left foot.

"Hmm," she said, without opening her eyes.

"Do you like more or less pressure?"

"Whatever you are doing is working just fine," Nina said.

It was too late to tell her date she wasn't into feet. If she mentioned it was all for the sake of her blog, it would look as if she were poking fun—just one more woman rejecting him.

"Tell me," she said. "Do you think it is easier to engage with people online? I mean, eventually they find out the truth, right?"

"That I'm a middle-aged, straight-laced banker into shoes?"

"The banker bit is a little hard to swallow, I admit. I can't really imagine you as straight-laced."

"Oh, I wear red suspenders under my jacket," he said. "Don't be fooled by the conservative appearance. Most bankers are into some kind of kink. It comes with the territory."

"And online?"

Candidate 166 made little thoughtful circles on her soles with his thumbs. "Online, I get to be light-hearted. I get to flirt and be decadent, and no one is the wiser."

"It's easy to forget yourself and get carried away when it's virtual," Nina said.

"Exactly. People tend to give in to their impulses before they catch themselves. Then, they put the brakes on. But you would be surprised to hear what they admit to in the safety of a chatroom."

"Oh, I have some idea," said Nina. "Having a thing for feet is not as weird as some of the stuff I've encountered. One guy I dated was into laundry detergent. He could only get aroused in basements."

"That's a pretty strange place to have a date."

"I made him meet me at a bar. No way I was going to his basement. Poor guy had to carry his detergent around in a little Ziploc bag that he kept in his briefcase. Come to think about it, he was also in finance."

"See? What did I tell you? Makes me sound positively normal."

Candidate 166 played with the straps of her garter, massaging the place on her thighs where they had pressed into her skin.

"You are very good with your hands," Nina said.

"Comes with the territory, dear. Are you comfortable? Here, turn this way."

She wanted so much to be aroused by this witty, charming man with his quiet self-assurance. But she felt miles away, as if she were suspended in air watching someone else act out her role.

Nina desired, expected even, that everyone she chatted with would experiment with different identities, like costume changes. That was the whole point of online transformation. Not to reconstruct truth, but to tweak it here and there, so that the fabric of reality wasn't instantly visible.

Rule three: If you've tried everything, cut your losses. Move on. Don't give your date false expectations and don't be tempted to feel pity. Would you want someone feeling sorry for you? Remember, there are too many fish to waste your time forcing a connection that isn't there.

"The thing is," Nina said. "We are all a little weird when you think about it. We're made of the same material and at the same time so different."

"Has anyone ever told you that you are an incurable romantic?"

Nina sat up, surprised.

"Relax, your secret is safe with me. More champagne?" He handed Nina the bottle and she took a swig.

"You see, that's why I like meeting people online," 166 said. That way they can't see me as I really am: bitter and silly and stupidly optimistic. Virtuality has a way of equalizing things. At least until we meet face-to-face. Then woman have no idea what to do with me."

"Believe me, I know."

"You are a wonderful exception. Do you mind if I take off my jacket?"

Nina shook her head, watching as Candidate 166 removed his tie and undid his top shirt button, folding his clothes into a neat pile and placing them in the seat in front of them.

In another life, they could have been friends—maybe even lovers. Given the right circumstances, who knows what would have happened? But in her 365-Date challenge there was no room for contemplation or regret. Go out with a man. Write about him. Move on.

"You know," she said. "The masquerade ball is great while it lasts, but eventually the masks have to come off."

"Why? People will only scatter like cockroaches into the shadows," he said, his fingers tracing long patterns on her calves.

Nina put her hand on top of his. "We say we want truth but the truth is we're afraid. We're afraid of what we'll find underneath all those layers of intrigue."

"I'm not afraid," he said. "I know who you are."

In the darkness, her eyes glistened. "And who am I?"

"A sad, lonely, misunderstood shoe freak, like me."

Perhaps tonight I am, she thought.

"So what happens now? I couldn't bear it if we connected and I lost you."

"Let's not think about that now. Let's focus on the present."

"Sorry. I've probably ruined the moment," he said.

"Not at all," she replied.

In his Mercedes, with her legs stretched across his lap, Nina let him unfasten her stockings from her garters. And afterwards, when he wept over her feet, she let him do that too.

FROGMAN

IT WAS ONLY while standing at one of the busiest airports in the country, waiting for a boyfriend she had never seen before, that the absurdity of Charlotte's situation began to make itself apparent. Armed with only a generic description—sandy hair, blue eyes, crooked smile—she set about scanning the passengers, wondering which one he was.

Charlotte had read that in the early, heady days of the Internet, it was not uncommon for people to fly thousands of miles across the world with no clue as to what their paramours looked like. Nowadays you were expected to ask for photos, videos, even a Skype account, so you could speak to each other in real time.

Nina Parks, author of the The Ultimate Guide to Finding Love on the Internet blog, suggested that when chatting, one should look beyond appearances and focus on the more important aspects, so when Charlotte met Andrés, she told him not to bother sending a photo. In her limited e-dating experience, physical descriptions tended to be highly exaggerated anyway. If they didn't have unrealistic expectations of one another there was less chance for disappointment.

The night before Andrés' flight, she called him at home.

"I have a feeling when we look into one another's eyes, we'll know," she whispered. "We'll know instinctively without words, doubts, or cardboard signs. But in case it all fails, what colour are your eyes?"

"Blue," he said. "My eyes are blue."

"What shade? Claudia Schiffer or Paul Newman?"

"Is there a difference? And why are you whispering?"

"Because it's romantic," Charlotte said, although there was nothing romantic about being folded up in the linen closet with the door closed, so Tom, her husband, couldn't hear her conversation.

"Schiffer," he said. "My eyes are Schiffer blue. How will I recognize you?"

"I'll be wearing a beret. Raspberry. Like in the Prince song."

"I can't wait to see you," he murmured and Charlotte held the receiver close to her chest.

At the airport, she examined her face in the bathroom mirror, enumerating her good and bad points and hoping the positives outweighed the negatives. Part of her was worried that Andrés might not find her appealing enough. A bigger part worried that it didn't matter to him. He liked her enough that a few flaws and imperfections weren't going to put him off. Somehow, this made Charlotte more nervous than the thought that he might not be attracted to her. She tried to control her shaky hands so she could brush her hair.

This is your last chance, she told her reflection. You can still eject from the pilot's seat. Make your choice. Go back home to your husband and stop meeting men online. Or risk it all and hope virtual love is every bit as wonderful as you hope it will be.

"Take a chance, dear," said an elderly woman washing her hands at the other sink. "You're meeting someone, aren't you? I can tell. Listen, don't spend your life wondering. Don't be guided by fear. Take a chance."

Charlotte glanced at the woman, wondering how she knew. Was it really that obvious? And would she still give her the same advice if the woman knew Charlotte was planning to cheat on her husband with a man twelve years younger than her? *Hussy.* That's what she would call her. A hussy.

"Thank you," Charlotte said, shoving her hairbrush into her bag.

She knew the first time she read his description that she liked him. Andrés was a writer. Chilean. Twenty-six years old. In his spare time, he edited a small but well-respected publication and he volunteered at a school for underprivileged kids.

Charlotte sent him a private message and he replied instantly, inviting her to a chatroom where they discussed literature.

Andrés: So who are your favourite Latin American writers?

Charlotte: Cortazar, Borges. Puig. I love *Heartbreak Tango.*

Andrés: *Argentines.* Figures. Who else?

Charlotte: Gabriel Garcia Marquez.

Andrés: Realismo Magical? Disqualified.

Charlotte: Wait. How can you disqualify Marquez?

Andrés: The same goes for Mario Vargos Llosa, in case he was next on your list. Don't you know any writers from Chile?

Charlotte: Allende. Pablo Neruda.

Andrés: Ay, Dios, they don't count.

Charlotte: Aren't they from Chile?

Andrés: Correction. Allende was born in Peru. Peru is NOT Chile.

Charlotte: And Neruda? I'm sure he's Chilean.

Andrés: Yes, but *everybody* knows Neruda. He's like the poetry equivalent of a Coca-Cola.

Charlotte: That's ridiculous.

Andrés: How about Dorfman, Donoso, Sepulveda? Have you read David Rosenmann?

Charlotte: I've never heard of them.

Andrés: You only read books that are popular?

Charlotte: Well yes, how else would I know they exist?

Andrés: Typical.

Charlotte: Wait a minute. You can't find it objectionable that I've not gotten around to reading every obscure writer on your list.

Andrés: Dorfman is not obscure!

Charlotte: I get it. You want someone that's a literary snob. If that is the case, I better go and find someone with more pedestrian reading tastes.

Andrés: No need to apologize. We were having an interesting discussion about accessible writing, no? You must be more patient and not lose your temper when you are in the wrong. You pretend to be open and friendly, but you are not very flexible. A body is supposed to be flexible.

Charlotte: Excuse me? First you complain that I don't read widely enough, now you insult me?

Andrés: I meant *cuerpo* as in person. Not as in your body. I don't know what that looks like, but my imagination is suddenly, *como se dice*, 'aroused'. You have to forgive my English. It is not always perfect.

Charlotte: Neither is your system of classification. According to Wikipedia, Dorfman was born in Buenos Aires.

Andrés: Perhaps on paper, yes, but spiritually he is Chilean. He spent his life in Santiago. He is one of us. Not an Argie. You may have predictable tastes, Charlie, but at least you are observant, no?

Charlotte: Gee, thanks. Listen, this Dorfman of yours may be brilliant or he may be overrated, despite what you say. I'll make my own choices. I don't appreciate being told what I should like.

Andrés: You misunderstand. There is validity in Marquez, even Allende. I was trying to say that not all literature comes from the same place. And not all Latin Americans are *Magical*.

Charlotte: You can say that again. I better go.

Andrés: Wait. Do you know what is happening between us? Are you familiar with the term *cuestión de piel?* It is a feeling you get after touching someone. You are never sure why—only that there is an intense feeling. Electrical. Instant. Your stomach churns, blood pumps, your skin is aware that something extraordinary is happening.

Charlotte: Except we haven't touched.

Andrés: No, not yet.

Charlotte stopped typing and stared at her screen. Her cheeks were flushed and her heart was pounding so loudly, she was glad Tom wasn't around. They had become one of those couples who spent their evenings on his/her laptops doing different things: Tom, downstairs locked in his office and Charlotte upstairs talking to Latin American men who believed in virtual love at first sight.

How she could get emotional about someone she had only spoken to for less than an hour? And he was bossy. She barely knew him and already they'd had their first argument. This is a one-time deal, she told herself, even while asking Andrés to elaborate on *cuestión de piel.*

Andrés: Virtually, this sensation exists as well. My new book is about the fascinating duality of the mind versus the body. I mean, how can you physically feel something when you are not actually feeling anything?

Charlotte: Well, whatever it is, I'm sure it is not what you think.

Andrés: Ah, I knew it. I knew you felt something too. Despite our differences, I think we are going to get on very well.

There must have been 250 people on the flight and Charlotte checked out every one, even the women. What if Andrés met someone else on the plane? That happened to blogger Nina Parks. Her callous snake of a date actually approached her with another woman in tow, saying it was fate, and who could rightly blame fate?

Charlotte would die if that ever happened to her. She could not imagine meeting and then losing Andrés in one-fell swoop. The thought of it made her feel wobbly. A handsome man walked past, stopped, and asked if she needed help. His eyes were dark blue and she tried to work out if the shade was closer to Newman than Schiffer.

"Andrés?" she said, looking up at him hopefully.

"No," said the man. "I'm Patrick. Are you OK? You look a little lost."

"I'm fine, thank you. Just waiting on my boyfriend."

He gave her a strange look. "Don't you know what he looks like? Have you been keeping your eyes closed the entire time?"

Charlotte forced a smile and walked away.

The airport lounge was almost empty, except for a young couple making out, a family with a little boy who refused to unglue himself from the window, and a man seated in the row behind the couple. At first Charlotte didn't notice him, as he was hidden behind a magazine. It couldn't be Andrés. It couldn't be. He was far too young, looking all of nineteen. Also his hair was ridiculous, combed back in a 1940s pompadour, perhaps to conceal a case of premature balding. She tried to remember if Andrés had ever mentioned his hair.

From Charlotte's vantage point, she couldn't determine the colour of his eyes. He turned toward her for a millisecond, squinted, and then returned to his magazine, slouching in his seat until he was practically invisible. Even if by chance that was Andrés (and that was highly improbable) he would have been looking for her, not sitting there idly reading. This guy didn't even seem curious.

She breathed a sigh of relief and wondered what to do next. Could she have missed Andrés in the crowd of passengers? He was probably waiting outside for her, wondering why she hadn't shown up. As she walked toward the exit, she passed the man with the pompadour who slightly resembled actor Steve Buscemi. Strike that, he looked more like a sickly frog, bulbous and pale with that oil-slick hair. Frogman didn't look up, just kept turning pages. Charlotte noted that his hands were delicate, almost feminine. She recalled a recent conversation where she told Andrés that she had worked since the age of 16. At college, she held down two jobs to support herself, one of them as a waitress.

"I don't understand," he said. "Didn't your parents help you out?"

"Of course they did. But working taught me to be financially independent."

"Charlie, the concept of financial independence is a vicious lie perpetuated by those who want to enslave you and keep you spending instead of doing something creative. Be revolutionary instead. Mindless occupations devour your soul."

She was getting used to conversations like this, which she put down to Andrés' youth and inexperience. Of course he would see things in his idealistic way. She bristled when he told her that well-brought up women should not engage in menial labour. There was such a class divide in Latin America. But things were different in the US. Still, part of what made Andrés so appealing was that he saw the world in a completely new and refreshing way.

"If you could only see my hands, Charlie. They are the hands of a poet; a philosopher."

"Well, we can't all sit around philosophizing. Besides, there is nothing wrong with a good work ethic, Andrés."

"Ethics are fine. I have no problem with ethics. I just don't like the idea of exploitation."

"So am I to take it that you've never worked a real job in your entire life?"

"I am at the library all day and I have my writing at night. I need only enough money to eat. I am not greedy. You Americans take pride in working for work's sake. You are not a peon."

"And you are not landed gentry."

"I am an *artist*. I must make time for my projects. I do not want to fry anyone's burgers or throw away garbage or pick fruit so I can buy games and plasma TVs and other things I don't need. Why should I be part of the system when money is the problem?"

"So what do you do if you are broke? Pawn your Dorfman collection? Would that even raise enough for a bottle of wine?"

"I don't write for money. You know that. Or maybe you don't understand because you are naïve and know little of the real world."

Andrés was the one who didn't understand. He thought life was like one of his books. He would be more shocked at seeing Tom's collection of technical gadgets and Star Wars memorabilia than he would at finding out Charlotte had a husband. Likewise, Tom would be less outraged to find she had taken a lover, than if she suggested he get rid of his materialistic trappings.

Until now she had viewed herself as different from her husband and her friends, more open-minded and liberal, but around Andrés she became conservative, almost anti-intellectual.

Despite her boyfriend's disdain for consumerism, he was eager to experience life in America.

"I've booked my ticket to see you. Now we'll have time together, like we planned."

"You're coming next month?" said Charlotte, alarmed. She had been working up the nerve to tell Tom she was going to Chile with some teachers at her school.

"Isn't it a wonderful surprise? Charlie, what's wrong? Don't you want to see me?"

"I thought we were going to wait until the summer."

"You are not happy," he said.

"I am. It's just that I told you about my roommate. She doesn't like visitors and I'm really up to my ears in work. It's a bad time."

"I understand and I don't want to make you anxious. I will be grateful for whatever time you can spare for me. I will be staying with a compatriot, but don't worry. We will have plenty of opportunity to see one another."

"How long are you staying?"

"Three months. But don't worry about entertaining me. I will be writing while you are at work and getting to know the city. We can be together in the evenings. And during the nights, obviously."

A few days later, Charlotte visited her sister to tell her the news. They sat in Rachel's newly decorated living room overlooking the lake. Everything was white. White carpets, white walls, white furniture. It was like a waiting room in a dentist's office.

"Let me get this straight, not only are you having an affair, but your soon to be lover has no clue you are married?"

"Rachel, please don't use the word *lover*. It's so 1970s."

"It certainly fits your farcical dilemma."

"Look, I didn't come here to be ridiculed."

"Well, it's difficult not to Charlotte, when you insist on making stupid decisions. Why weren't you upfront with him from the start?"

"I don't know. I wanted to be, but he was so eager. I couldn't tell him."

"How do you think he's going to feel now? He's coming here to be with you in the dead of winter and you aren't even available."

"I'm going to tell Tom I have a sick friend. That will buy me a few nights. I don't think he would even notice."

"Charlotte, have you thought of the possibility—I don't like to say this— but what if Andrés is one of those people?"

"What people?"

"You know. An *immigrant* using you to get his visa? Don't give me that outraged look. You read about it all the time, predators moving in on hapless women."

There it was. Rachel never hinted at anything if she could aim directly.

"Andrés isn't that kind of guy. He doesn't care about money or visas. He cares about writing."

"And you, apparently."

"It's the truth. He doesn't want to live here. Some people prefer their own countries, you know. Besides, what do we have offer him here that's so great? A job as a dishwasher or a gardener? He's a fucking poet."

"Please don't take that tone with me, I'm only trying to help."

"Why would anyone want to subject themselves to our way of life if they don't have to? Part of what I love about him is how much he clings to his ideals."

"In that case," Rachel's voice dropped an octave. "What do you think is going to happen when he finds out you are married? Charlotte. Don't cry. Here, take a tissue. You are getting snot on my new couch."

They sat looking at the white-capped waves from the living room window.

"You are going to have to tell Tom."

"I know. But he's hard to pin down. He's always busy at work or on his computer."

"Well, write him a goddamn email or send him a telegram or something. Don't get stuck in a position where you are reacting instead of being proactive." Rachel worked as a consultant for a well-known corporation and her speech was often peppered with business truisms. "You need to be open and transparent for the good of the partnership," she said. "No matter if you can't stand your husband anymore. You have to have full disclosure."

"You're right. I'll tell Tom as soon as I can."

"So, you really care about this Andrés?"

Charlotte blew her nose. "I do. He's so different from the other men I met on Match Made in Heaven. Remember the boat guy and the one who was a hand model? Andrés gets me. He's smart and funny. He has a great personality.

"You know that's code for 'hideous loser who can't get a date in the real world', right?"

"Come on Rach."

"What about your cultural differences."

"We don't have any. Besides, plenty of people from different backgrounds get married."

"Marriage!" Rachel stood up, the veins in her neck pronounced. "Unbelievable!"

"I didn't mean us. Andrés is not conventional. He doesn't believe in bourgeois institutions that strangle you with restrictions and unreasonable demands."

Her sister sighed. "This may come as a total surprise to you, Charlie, but people will do and say anything to get what they want. Even when they are in love." She paused for a moment. "*Especially* when they are in love. You obviously have no idea what you want. But decide soon, otherwise you are going to end up bitter and disillusioned, and you don't want that."

"Is that how you felt after Donald left? Disillusioned?

"We weren't talking about me," said her sister smoothing out her skirt. "For years, I've listened to you ramble on about how unhappy you are. How unfair everything is. How everyone has someone to love except you. Now you have two people to choose from. Either start taking responsibility for your decisions or keep screwing up your life. You are only hurting yourself."

She walked out of the room, leaving Charlotte alone on the pristine couch.

***

Charlotte walked to the taxi rank. A few moments later, the man she'd previously seen in the passenger lounge joined the line. His skin had a greenish tinge further emphasizing his amphibious looks. He was short. His trousers so small, they looked as if he'd purchased them in the children's department. That man wasn't Andrés. He looked too beaten and downtrodden by life. The kind of person you passed on the street without a second glance.

"Unreal expectations of beauty and desire have ruined many budding relationships," She read in The Ultimate Guide to Finding Love Online. "If you want to discover a person's real essence, look in the deeper layers, beyond the surface of their skin."

"Do you know how blind people fall in love?" Charlotte had asked Andrés, explaining how porcupines make love. "Carefully. Very carefully."

"I do not understand this joke," he said.

"Don't worry. I will explain later."

Standing outside of the airport, the man, who may or may not have been Andrés, was picking at a pimple on his face. He caught her looking at him and stared back, as if she were a delicious insect. She felt an inexplicable twitch of revulsion. She guessed if people could fall in love at first sight, they could also develop instant antipathy.

"I am going to count to ten," Charlotte said to herself. "I am going to count to ten and if he turns away, he's not Andrés."

One, two, three. He was still looking.

Four, five, six. The line moved up.

Seven.

"Miss, are you waiting for a cab?"

Eight.

Charlotte jumped in. "Come on, come on, come on," she urged the driver.

Nine.

"It's bumper-to-bumper as far as the eye can see." He shrugged at the long row of stalled cabs, grid-locked in traffic for at least half a mile.

"Ten," she said out loud.

Frogman was still staring, watching her with his watery, sea anemone eyes.

Charlotte was sick with nerves, imagining her online lover caressing her with those soft, pasty hands. Kissing her with those bloated lips. But her true love was not a frog. He was a poet. An intelligent, interesting person that was everything she wanted from a man. Andrés inspired feelings she couldn't understand. That had to mean something. But where was he and why hadn't he found her yet? She tried to remember what she told him the previous evening. *I'll be wearing a raspberry-coloured beret.*

Charlotte reached up and touched her head. She must have left her hat in the airport bathroom when she was talking to that woman. She leaned against the worn seat of the cab. The driver was asking something, but she was too busy watching the man she was certain was not Andrés, moving slowly toward the taxi, dragging an enormous suitcase behind him. His bloated skin appeared blotchy in the sunlight, as if he had never ventured outside.

She had hoped that Andrés would free her from her relationship with Tom, providing a clean slate that was unmarred by expectation—a second chance at romance. And now here she was, trying to escape the airport because her boyfriend had turned out not to be a prince after all but a frog.

The decision not to send one another photographs had backfired. As much as Charlotte had tried to clear her head of expectations, the empty space she had saved for Andrés had been filled-in, her mind conjuring up a tousled-haired, sapphire-eyed, lanky writer to go with the personality she was so familiar with online.

The painfully short and inept Frogman had no place in her scenario—a painful reminder that reality was as far removed from fantasy as she was from herself at that very moment. Charlotte had been unable to keep her virtual space safe from her own prejudices. As a result, everything was wrong.

She felt a pang of sadness for the loss of Andrés, who was destined to stay in cyberspace where he belonged.

"If you truly want romance, go after it with your eyes wide open," wrote Nina Parks.

Hearing a loud thud, Charlotte turned to see the Frogman lunging for the bumper of the cab. He missed it entirely, flopping to the ground next to his suitcase. He lay there in a defeated hump.

"What are you waiting for? Go!" she shouted at the driver, hoping they'd leave the pale impostor on the ground where he belonged. But she had misjudged the Frogman. He rose to his feet, dusted himself off, and started running behind the taxi like something out of the Terminator. He moved pretty quickly for a tiny man, pumping his extremities in an exaggerated motion.

Charlotte watched as the Frogman gained speed, his amphibious mouth panting in, out, in out, like a bloated fish washed up on shore. His eyes, now that she could see them up close, were a startling shade of Claudia Schiffer blue.

As a long-time reader of your blog. I find myself agreeing with nearly everything you say and sometimes the truth is so startling, I feel as if you must be reading my diary. My query is regarding online relationships, more specifically about my virtual boyfriend.

I would very much like to meet him but I'm scared of what will happen—or what won't happen to be more precise. What if we don't like each other? What if he decides I'm not suitable? What if the connection is all in my head?

Just meet him, you say in your blog. But it isn't that easy. I'm not brave. I'm not good with new people. The last time I liked someone it turned out to be a disaster. Let's just say when I kissed my frog, he didn't turn into anything. He just stayed a frog. You can probably tell I've invested a lot in this relationship. I'm torn between my desire to meet or continue as we are.

Just to clarify, the idea of seeing him in person makes me weak in the knees. Not in a swooning Hollywood way, but in a rubber-legged, fall over and hit my head kind of way.

I have to confess that lately we are not as happy as we were before. The words are usually so perfect between us. I never have to lie or pretend I am something I am not. But it isn't enough. I feel him getting more and more restless. It's as if meeting is all that matters—not the countless conversations or the secrets we've shared.

Have we been marking time until our inevitable conclusion? Why has it become all about the physical? I'm afraid I've lost perspective. Please help shed some light on this. I eagerly await your response. Yours in confusion.

From: loveguru@ultimateguidetolove.com
To: Anonymous

Dear Confusion, yours is a fear that many couples experience when they've been chatting for a while, I'm afraid there's not much I can say that I've not said before, so bite the bullet and meet your virtual prince! To not do so might bring a premature end to your relationship and I'm sure you don't want that. Although, given what you've said, I think you may have to re-evaluate the importance of a physical relationship. Our urge as humans to seek one another out, to be together, to huddle for warmth, cannot be discounted as mere superficialities. Biological bodies are more than vehicles for hair and clothes. They make us feel safe, balanced, and ultimately, alive.

By the way, my new book *The Ultimate Guide To Finding Love Online* is coming out soon. It's an accompaniment to the blog and I hope you will read it, as it addresses the problems you've mentioned. I also advise you to try to meet your paramour in a place that isn't too loud or flashy. Preferably somewhere low-key and factor in plenty of time for both of you to feel at ease. Although it is natural to feel a little uncomfortable the first time. I wish you the best and let me know how it goes. Remember to read my book when it comes out at a bookstore near you.

The Online Love Guru

RAT MAZE

Nina Parks was introduced to the Internet during her first year at university. After meeting in the library and swearing her to secrecy, Jillian Jones took Nina three levels down to a dungeon-like lost room that only a handful of students knew about.

"Welcome to the Rat Maze," Jillian said with a flourish.

Once her eyes adjusted to the darkness, Nina saw they were not alone. The grim lab, surrounded by ancient computer terminals was crowded with students sitting on long wooden benches, the fluorescent backdrops from their screens tingeing their fingers and faces an unhealthy shade of green. The room was eerily quiet, except for the sound of keys clicking and the occasional stifled giggle or sigh.

"Why isn't anyone talking?" Nina asked.

"Trust me, they are," her classmate said in a stage whisper. "I've created an account for you. Here, I'll show you what to do." She hit a few keys rapidly and then a little slower, repeating her steps until Nina nodded. "You'll find the format a little weird at first, but you'll get used to it. Conversations on here aren't so different to normal ones."

"So this is what you do on Saturday nights?" Nina asked. "You hang out here?"

"Most evenings as well," said a boy two benches across from them.

"Mind your own business, Ben," Jillian said.

"Look around you," he said to Nina. "We're a bunch of die-hard addicts." He cracked his neck. "Everyone here is suffering some kind of after-effect symptom. Mike, over there, has carpal tunnel. Emma, on your other side, suffers from back pain and has to lie flat out on the floor to sleep at night. Rob hasn't had a hot meal in three months; he subsists on beef jerky and Mountain Dew. Jillian here, she'll tell you it's part of the package. But she'll leave off the migraines, insomnia and eye sprains." Ben punctuated each malady by cracking a knuckle. "And those are the physical symptoms. Don't get me started on the rest. Thing is, you don't notice until it's too late. By then you're a goner. BANG. *Addicted*."

"Okay Ben, she gets the point," said Jillian. "Don't let him scare you. Spend as long as you want down here. Just don't tell anyone about this place."

"Yeah, the Powers That Be don't want us chatting when we could be doing more productive things with our time." Ben raised his eyebrows meaningfully before going back to his screen.

Nina took to chat instantly. The girl who never fit in anywhere, who made only one friend in her four years of high school, finally felt as if she belonged. She would waltz into the Rat Maze, nod at the regulars and take a seat at the bench furthest from the door, content in the knowledge that here, she was accepted. It wasn't about her looks, which was a tiring subject Nina had no desire to engage in. This rapport was based on acknowledgement, some sort of secret clubhouse membership, where no one questioned why a pretty girl, who could date any guy she wanted, preferred to spend her evenings in a cold basement.

The chatters for the most part, weren't interested in her friendship or in starting conversations, for which Nina was grateful. In the Rat Maze everything that was worth happening, happened on screen.

—>Hello. Is anyone out there?

—>Hello? Can you read me?

Every time Nina sent out a message, she would get a rush of adrenalin in the pit of her stomach at the thought that someone, in another basement, in another school (possibly even in another continent) was reading her missives. She wondered if Alexander Graham Bell felt the same shock of recognition the first time he heard a tinny voice on the other end of the line. *Eureka.* A connection. Not just a progression of technology—another human being.

Before Nina's father left her and her mother for one of his students, he would spend his Saturdays down in the basement, drinking the two beers he allowed himself on weekends, and listening in on other people's conversations on his CB radio. Occasionally, he'd send out his own tentative message.

"This is Ranger007. Anyone out there?"

Whenever a strange voice emerged from the static to reply, he would excitedly shout "Eureka!" his voice resounding throughout the house.

"Ed, keep it down. We're trying to sleep," her mother Frankie would call out. And Nina, snug in her bed, would fall asleep to the voice of her father excitedly talking on his radio.

"So you prefer to spend your evenings chatting to robots than going out?" asked Frankie, who called her daughter every Sunday morning like clockwork.

"Ma, they're not cyborgs," Nina said. "They're real people. It's like talking on the telephone, except we type."

"You don't talk?"

"Yes. Online."

"And these guys you talk, I mean, *type* to on your computer, they go to your school?"

"No."

"How do you know them?"

"It's complicated."

"Well, which is it? Do you know them or don't you?"

"Yes, except in the physical sense."

Nina explained that meeting men online was not like visiting Narnia or some equally fantastical world that existed solely in her head.

"It's just a device, ma, a different way to meet people. Like being set-up by the neighbourhood matchmaker, but you know, electronically. Please don't get upset."

"Upset? Who's upset? I'm thrilled. Electronic men can't get you pregnant, right?"

"No, not yet," Nina said.

In 1994, people didn't fully understand the Internet. Years later, after it was used to replicate almost any transaction you could do in person, it still carried a social stigma. People asked Nina the same questions over and over again; refusing to believe that it was possible to be attracted to a person you had never seen before.

She wanted to tell them to stop being so close-minded, so accepting of convention. Only because something had been done a certain way for years did not guarantee its success. Especially when the current accepted form of meeting was often a drunken interchange in a crowded bar.

The people Nina chatted with weren't interested in her clothes or how she wore her hair. They expected her to talk about books and films, to be witty, interesting and smart. She jumped into electronic conversations with both feet, happy to flirt and tell jokes, to exchange her thoughts and open up in a way she had never been able to successfully pull off face-to-face. She couldn't remember the last time someone listened to the words coming out her mouth without being distracted by her physical appearance. It was refreshing to have a blank slate in place of a face and body.

Best of all, her fellow chatters understood that mad eureka moment. That moment when you connected with another person, realizing just for an instant that you were not completely alone.

One week after being introduced to the Rat Maze, Nina met Cypher. He was razor-sharp, moody and fanatically secretive, almost paranoid in his refusal to divulge details of his personal life. Nina wasn't privy to basic information, such as his real name or what city he was from. All she knew was that he lived alone with two cats: he didn't tell her their names either. Cypher treated all of her questions suspiciously, even the innocent ones. Despite these drawbacks, he possessed the two qualities Nina most desired in a boyfriend: he understood space, knowing instinctively when to disappear and when to resurface, and he wasn't demanding. He let her get on with her life without the intrusive, insecure demands other guys made.

Every time Nina raised the subject of meeting, Cypher asked if she found him lacking in some way, as if this kind of virtual relationship *in absentia* was perfectly normal. If she persisted, he disappeared for varying periods of time, never saying when he'd return.

Nina sat for hours in the Rat Maze, waiting for Cypher to come online. When she saw his nickname flash up on her screen, she felt a surge of electricity through her body like a double shot of espresso. When he didn't log in, she'd plunge into depression, her withdrawal symptoms so severe she would skip classes, meals, even baths, spending all her time waiting for him to reappear.

The more Cypher sidestepped her, the more Nina became obsessed with him. Pretty soon meeting was all she talked about, their conversations playing on a perpetual loop, until all their interactions sounded the same.

Cypher: So where were we?

Kallioppe: We were talking about meeting.

Cypher: So where did we leave off?

Kallioppe: Discussing where we were going to meet.

Cypher: I thought you understood. I'm not comfortable getting together right now.

Kallioppe: But we have to. We're in a state of déjà vu. We're in quicksand, falling fast. I need something tangible.

Cypher: I'm sorry. I can't talk right now. I have to run. Can we save this for later?

"Have you been here all night, junkie?" said Jillian, finding Nina asleep with her head on the keyboard one morning.

"I was studying, for an exam."

"Of course you were. Remember Nina, the first step is acceptance."

"Shut up, Jones, I don't have a problem."

"Oh yeah? How come you're down here all the time? How long have you been wearing that shirt? When was the last time you had food that didn't come from the vending machine?"

"Don't preach to me. You're down here all the time too."

"Yeah, well at least I admit I have a problem." Jillian handed her a Snickers bar. "Breakfast of Champions," she said. "So, is he even worth it, Nina? I mean, how much do you really know about him?"

"What are you getting at?"

"Let me ask you this: does he call you in the middle of the night? Does he whisper? Does he act sneaky?"

Nina had known Cypher for four months, but they had never talked on the phone. In fact, if she took every single conversation they had and strung them up side-by-side like washing on a clothesline, the total sum would amount to no more than a few hours.

"You think he's married?" Nina asked Jillian.

"I'm not saying for sure. But I knew a guy once who never called because he said talking on the phone made him uncomfortable and brought out his stutter."

"Yeah, so?" said Nina.

"So, I found out later he was a sales rep. His job required him to be on the phone all day, and the discomfort he referred to was his wife, Rita."

Nina looked at her for a few moments. "You made that story up, didn't you?"

"Maybe, but the point still stands," said Jillian. "You know it isn't real, right? I mean you are. I am. This dungeon is real, but what you're feeling isn't love, or whatever, It's the Rat Maze," she shrugged. "Have you ever been to Vegas?"

"I'm an addict, I get it, OK? What does that have to do with anything, Jones?"

"Hear me out. Before my dad became a minister, he was a gambler. He used to say that the thing that most got to him, was that the casinos didn't have any windows or clocks. You just sat there playing for hours, disconnected from the rest of the world, with no awareness of time or space. Don't be like all the other people down here. Don't get sucked in by this place. It's an illusion. Watch."

Jillian sauntered over to the door, looked around the lab and then pulled the light switch. Nina watched as the room erupted into chaos, the horrified students shielding their eyes and screaming, as if they would combust in the light. Jillian gave Nina an I-told-you-so smile, before turning the light off, leaving the chatters in darkness.

Nina wrote out a pros and cons list, detailing each point in the back of her English notebook.

+Cypher was constant like the tide. No matter how upset she was or what she wrote him in a moment of anger, he would eventually pop back up on her computer, as if nothing had transpired. That kind of clean-slate perspective was refreshing.

–Cypher was a reluctant time-impaired narcissist. With him there was no past and no future. Only the present existed, suspended like a fly in amber.

+Cypher was a wordsmith. Yes, he was aloof and reluctant, but he was also deeply poetic, sending her beautifully descriptive emails, which she would read and reread, again and again in the dim light of the Rat Maze. He wasn't a great conversationalist, but letter-wise, she couldn't ask for more.

–Talking with Cypher was like being trapped in a funhouse. Not that he was a circus freak or a figment of her imagination. But he had a way of distorting reality.

But why did he keep disappearing and more importantly, where did he go? Most guys Nina chatted with online would kill to meet her in person, but not Cypher. At first, Nina happily filled in the blanks, creating different scenarios that explained his whole secrecy act, imagining him as a hacker, secret agent or political warrior. But more and more, she was beginning to believe that Cypher was the kind of person who always found an excuse to maintain his distance. He was, without question, socially dysfunctional, but maybe it wasn't his job that kept him away. Maybe he was married with kids, or in prison. Maybe he just didn't care.

Cypher: I know I'm asking a lot of you, but trust me, in a few months things will get better. I'll be able to explain what I'm not at liberty to say right now. Can you wait that long?

Kallioppe: We aren't moving forward. We're stuck in the same place. What you don't get is that I'm not the same person I was when you first met me. I can't wait around forever for you to pop back into my life.

Cypher: I'm sorry. It has never been my intention to hurt you. Can we start over?

Kallioppe: I don't think so.

Cypher: Because I won't meet you?

Kallioppe: Look, you are always leaving abruptly, with no explanation, no clue when you'll be back. With you, everything is in a state of transience.

Cypher: Give me time. I know I have no right to ask, but I'm asking anyway.

Kallioppe: We've chatted for months and I still don't know your real name. I'm sorry, but I'm tired of spending time with someone who isn't interested in me. You know what? I think you're full of shit. You don't know how to get close to anyone so you make excuses.

Cypher: I'm sorry you feel this way. I'm even sorrier that you won't allow me to defend myself. Can't you just appreciate what we have?

Kallioppe: NO," said Nina. "Because we don't have anything.

She logged off chat and sat in the Rat Maze, watching her fellow students. The computer lab, once so full of possibilities, now seemed cramped and depressing. There was the usual eerie silence and the sickly green from the screens, but she had never noticed the overpowering smell of dank basement, the odour of pheromones, sweat, and God only knows what else. Nina, who didn't know what day it was, and who had stopped going to classes, wondered what else she had missed, as she sat there night after night engrossed in her conversations. Jones was right about it being an illusion, but Nina wasn't an addict. She could walk away any time she wanted. She took a pair of cat-eye sunglasses from her backpack. "Hasta la Vista, Rat Maze," she said, waltzing out of the dungeon into the spring sunshine.

TERMINAL ROMANCE

No MATTER HOW much Jillian Jones had mentally prepared herself, meeting her online boyfriend for the first time came as a shock. "I was beginning to think you'd stood me up," Harlan said, when he saw her enter the café. He smiled, his eyes taking in her face and hair and resting on her lips. "Come on, sit down. Have something to drink. You look as if you need it."

She wished someone had warned her that the moment she had anticipated for so long would render her almost speechless, so that for the first fifteen minutes, all she did was nod at Harlan whenever he asked a question. In truth, she had no idea what he was saying. All she could hear was the explosion of colours, textures and forms that made up her boyfriend. For his part, Harlan watched her calmly, sipping his tea as if he nothing unusual were happening. As if this was the way people met all the time.

Jillian fidgeted with the menus and when the waitress whisked them away, with the sugar packets on the plate beside her. "Can you believe it took us seven months to get here?" Harlan said. To Jillian it sounded like: *SW!(£@! Like the sound parents made in the Peanuts animations.

Perhaps exchanging photos would have muted the initial impact, slowed it down somewhat so that she could process it better. Not that a still could ever convey the reality of Harlan's mouth or the shadows under his cheeks. No matter how much synchronicity they'd shared online, in person, their language was stilted and choppy, like in a silent film where the dialogue on the screen never matches the actors' lips.

(Chat Log: two months before meeting)

Jillian: If we met in person, there wouldn't be this level of expectation. Doing it in reverse order is tricky. You already know me, even though you haven't seen me.

Harlan: So we jump right in, like in a cold pool. Don't overthink it. Let's meet now.

Jillian: Right this minute?

Harlan: Yep. I'll hop on a plane. You can meet me at the terminal. What do you say?

Jillian: I don't want to meet at an airport. Airports are the least romantic places in the world. Why not a train station or a bus depot? Somewhere more atmospheric.

Harlan: Wait, why are we getting sidetracked? I thought the important thing was seeing one another?

Jillian: I want it to be perfect.

Harlan: Yes and each time we delay meeting, it gets worse.

Jillian: Wouldn't you like to meet in a place where thousands of passionate encounters have taken place? Where drama and pathos are etched into the very walls?

Harlan: You want pathos?

Jillian: I want it to be memorable, like a scene from a film: there you are, running along the platform, the station buzzing with porters loading trunks, men wearing hats and looking at their pocket watches. Through the foggy haze, you catch sight of her, the perfect woman, teetering away. She stops, turns, and looks at you for a millisecond. That's all it takes. Suddenly you can't bear the thought that she's about to steal out of your life forever. The poignancy of that moment is palpable—what do you do?

Harlan: To continue your *scenario noir*, this hulky protagonist, having denied his romantic inclinations his entire life, takes on your challenge, if only to reveal the momentous truth about himself in the process. The truth is that he's chasing Mystery Woman, not because of her perfumed allure, or because she might just be (gasp) his last stab at love. No, he is running after her based on the way her legs look in those stockings.

Jillian: Typical. No wonder she's running away.

Harlan: Correction. She's not running away, she's hoping he'll follow. And, BTW, why are elaborate, embarrassing heroics the only way to prove a man's love? Can't she take his word for it?

Jillian: No.

Harlan: So what you are saying is you want me to run after you?

Jillian: You don't have a single romantic bone in your body, do you?

Harlan: I do, but it makes it difficult to hobble across the platform with any effectiveness, if you get my drift.

Jillian: Tell me how meeting over coffee in an anonymous airport compares to my scenario?

Harlan: It will be perfect because you will be there.

Jillian: Sweet, but I still want some ambience or tender gesture to make the transition a little easier. In case it turns out to be a terminal romance.

Harlan: A what?

Jillian: A significant but ultimately doomed encounter between lovers. A poignant break-up in a place that epitomizes missed encounters, like the Empire State Building.

Harlan: Weren't Meg Ryan and Tom Hanks in a film like that?

Jillian: You're thinking about the one where they meet on email.

Harlan: This one featured a character obsessed with death who falls in love with a chirpy blonde. I think she has a virtual orgasm at the airport.

Jillian: In a deli, not an airport.

Harlan: So let's meet there. You can have what she was having. Jillian, if we don't do this, we'll be doomed to navigate endlessly around one another in cyberspace like Darth Vader.

Jillian: See, you haven't met anyone online before, so you think it will go smoothly. What if it doesn't? What if we're tongue-tied? What if we hate the sight of each other so much that it is impossible to think of anything but immediate escape? And all because the person sitting across from you, the princess you dreamed of all those months, turned out to be an ugly frog.

Harlan: If we happen not to hit it off right away (and let me say for the record, I don't think that will be the case) we'll step back like mature adults and decide what to do. Look, we've had all these months to get to know one another. If you happen to be a troll, I'll kiss you.

Jillian: You're thinking of a frog, not a troll. Trolls don't turn into princesses. Trolls don't turn into anything. They stay trolls.

Harlan: Well I happen to like trolls. If you resemble one, I'll desire you all the more. Have I ever told you about my secret fetish for fairy tale characters?

Jillian: Sick, Harlan. Sick.

Harlan: We won't know any of this until we have our first date. In a worst-case scenario, we'll go home, gnash our teeth and when it's bearable, try to be friends. We can't lose. Even if our date is disastrous, I promise I'm not going to disappear from your life.

Jillian: What if there is no physical attraction between us? Worse, what if there is no physical *possibility*?

Harlan: Take a deep breath. Done? Take another one. We have to do this. Jillian, if we're serious about one another, we have to meet. You always say it takes a while for the mind to catch up with the body. If the process isn't immediate, we'll take baby steps while we wait for the universe to unfold.

Jillian should have explained to Harlan that the universe had a history of denying her what she most wanted. Despite her warnings, he continued to let the nuances of virtuality escape through his hands like sand from a broken hourglass.

"Well. We did it," Harlan said.

Under cover of the Formica table, Jillian wiped her sweaty palms on her skirt. So many conversations and she couldn't think of a single thing to say to the man she'd been chatting to for months.

Maybe we've run out of things to talk about, she told herself. Maybe we've already covered everything there is and now we wait for the shocking jolt of physicality to kick in. Say something clever, Jillian. Don't sit there like a big lump. Say something clever.

"Are you jet lagged?" was all she came up with. "I know a really good remedy. Turkey. High in tryptophan, which forms serotonin, which makes melatonin. You've heard of melatonin right? The stuff your body manufactures at night while you sleep? It keeps you in sync. So when you get home later tonight you should probably have a turkey sandwich and a glass of milk."

"Turkey, huh?"

Jillian nodded with the assured conviction of someone who knew what she was talking about, even though she'd stolen the turkey tip from a travel magazine she'd found in the cafe.

"Well then, I'll have to remember to carry a bird on me at all times," he said.

"No need. I got you this." She handed him a fridge magnet of a smiling gobbler.

"You shouldn't have. Really."

When he took the magnet from her, she noticed that his hand was trembling. She felt relieved and touched that he was as nervous as she was.

One of the most daunting aspects of meeting face-to-face was coming to terms with the unfamiliar gestures and movements of each other's bodies. Connected, as they had been online, the choreography of Harlan's physical self was a foreign language that Jillian didn't speak. Her knowledge of him amounted to a database of statistics, details and descriptions, which in themselves amounted to nothing. Harlan's essence was in those lips of his, twitching behind his coffee cup. His real secrets buried in the follicles of hair that lay pliant under the watch on his right wrist.

Watching him doing perfectly ordinary things, such as stirring sugar into his mug, was a confirmation that despite everything she had said online, they had turned out to be so uncomfortable around one another. The truth of their predicament provoked a surge of conflicting emotions in Jillian. She wanted to cry, to run away, to hurl herself into his arms and ask why he didn't recognize her. She couldn't bear the blank but kind look in his eyes. If only she could go back in time, armed with her new knowledge. Would things be any different?

Harlan broke a ginger snap neatly in two and offered her half. She shook her head and took a large sip of coffee, burning her tongue.

"Hey, careful there," he said. "Are you all right?"

Jillian nodded and wiped her eyes. It was hard to look at him. His face was both familiar and entirely new. She wanted to stare at him, tracing every line on his face, memorizing and comparing it to what she knew of him already. She focused instead on a couple awaiting their flight. The girl's leg was casually thrown across her boyfriend's, his arm resting lightly on her back. Jillian was filled with envy at the ease the couple had with one another. To think that after all this time she and Harlan were still virtual strangers. It was too sad to bear. She took another sip of scalding coffee.

She remembered the first time she spoke to him on the phone. He hadn't warned her he would call. She hadn't even given him her number. She was in the bath and when the phone wouldn't stop ringing, she climbed out and barked, "This better be good."

"It definitely sounds like it will be," said a deep sexy voice.

Jillian stood very still, a pool of water collecting on the floor in her hallway. "Who is this?"

"You still don't know?" he said. "Let me give you a hint. Yesterday, at approximately 1:30am you confessed a secret love affair with coffee-flavoured ice cream."

"Harlan?"

"Unless you've been chatting with other guys about your food fantasies."

"Me with my food fantasies, you with your fairy tales."

"When you answered the phone, I expected you to sound like HAL," Harlan said. "Not the sweet union of Jessica Rabbit and Eartha Kitt. You have the most amazing voice, Jillian. God, I love your voice."

"Well," Jillian said, holding out both her arms to encompass the table, the café and the terminal. "I didn't think we'd ever meet. But here we are, face to face. And I was right. It is truly awful, isn't it? I bet you're thinking it wasn't such a great idea to meet after all. I should have placed money on it." She was joking. Hoping Harlan would laugh and the lump in her throat would disappear.

Gone was the rapport, the romantic tension, the crazy passion that fuelled their late-night dialogues. In its place was gentle consideration and the careful looks they gave each another when they thought the other wasn't looking. Jillian missed Harlan's raunchy playfulness. His irreverence. He sat across from her, minding his manners as if she were his granny.

Online, they had been hyper-attuned to every little nuance. In person, they plodded along, their spider-senses switched off. First meets were always filled with false expectations, subtleties that were almost impossible to catch over text and telephone. It was normal to feel confused, if not outright cheated when you didn't instantly click, forgetting that it wasn't so much failure to launch, as it was surface newness.

"We talked about it for so long," he said. "It's strange to see you actually here in front of me. All those hours I spent imagining how you would look and here you turn out to be... *you*. But in a way, you are also less you, if that makes sense?" He placed one hand over hers and held it there for a few seconds.

She told herself to keep realistic expectations. This was, after all, the monumental 'First Date'. Perhaps the second would be better, and so on, until they eased into a pattern that matched what they'd had online.

"Something is missing. I don't know what it is," Harlan said. His eyes when they met hers, looked incredibly sad.

Jillian felt her heart fall to the floor. It slithered its miserable way across the airport, until it was trampled by a crowd of people racing to catch their flights. Why hadn't he listened to anything she had said? There were no guarantees when it came to the great reveal. She knew without him having to say it, that there would be no second date.

They announced Harlan's flight an hour later. He told Jillian he'd booked a short layover so as not to pressure her. But she wondered if he would have changed his flight if things with her had gone in a different direction. He seemed relieved. Eager to go. Just as well. Other than repeating how surprised they were to finally meet, they hadn't said much more. Earlier, she had noticed him glancing at an attractive blonde wearing a blue dress and carting a wheelie suitcase. It was just a flicker, a minute movement of his eyes over her body, but long enough for the blonde to notice and answer back with her own Morse code response.

There was no logical answer to why attraction happened or hadn't in this case. Perhaps they had waited too long between meeting online and meeting in person, or maybe like one of those romance films Jillian claimed to hate but secretly loved, they were star-crossed lovers, never destined to be.

She thought of all those conversations where they talked about the day they'd finally sit across from one another. All those late-night eroticisms, the mounting desperation. It had all come to nothing. She wasn't a princess. She wasn't even a frog. She was sub-troll. Not ugly, not beautiful, just unworthy of Harlan's contemplation. At least if she had been a troll, Harlan's apathy would have made sense. He thought her pretty, but it wasn't enough. He was expecting more and she didn't know what to say to make things better. Part of her wanted to soothe him. A bigger part wanted to slap him, to tell him to snap out of it. She had braced herself against rejection but not indifference.

She searched in her handbag for anything: a breath mint, lipstick, a pencil, just please, please, not a tissue. Finding a tissue when she needed it the most, would be the thing to trigger the tears. She didn't want to cry in front of him. She could not stand it if he showed her pity. That would be the final straw.

Jillian kept her head down, biting her lip and willing herself not to break down. She had both dreamed and dreaded this moment for so long, at last throwing aside doubt and allowing herself a little hope. Hope that their date would be like one of those films where the lovers ran across a field of flowers to embrace, able to recognize each other, even at a distance and cling. Just cling to one another until the dreaded terror was assuaged. But this was not the *Summer of Love*. This was *Fight Club*. Months of friendship and love and lust and they were still wary strangers, circling one another in combat.

When Jillian finally stopped rummaging in her purse, Harlan hoisted his carry-on, adjusted the strap of his laptop bag and gave her a polite smile.

"I have to go. They're calling my flight."

"Don't forget your turkey," she said pointing to the table where the magnet lay forgotten among the sugar packets.

He picked it up gingerly and placed it into his pocket.

"I'm sorry," he said not looking at her. Jillian nodded, not trusting herself to speak.

"You'd better go," she finally said.

"Yes," he said, not moving.

She stood up and right there, in the middle of the crowded airport, looked directly into Harlan's eyes for the first time—the man she'd been in love with for the better part of a year.

"You underestimated the way physicality works," she said. "The way it can creep up on you and undo all the words you've said."

"Look Jillian. I know this is awkward," Harlan stammered. "I didn't know meeting would be like this. You warned me but I had no idea. I feel so inadequate. I need to think about it. I wish we could discuss this, but it's better for both of us if I go now. Can we talk later?"

Harlan thought that exchanging a few sentences in person would tell him everything he needed to know about her. He'd been so willing to give up their intimate conversations and the trade-off had been what? A stilted, pitiful, conclusion. The desperation of waiting for her lover to notice her as a real living, breathing, woman.

"Have a safe flight."

She smoothed the lapels of his jacket and then reached over and placed her mouth against his. Jillian kissed him softly, breathing in his freshly shaved skin, then brushed her lips slowly from cheek to his earlobe and stopped, as if preparing to say something worthy of remembering, something that would haunt Harlan for the rest of his days.

"You'll never know," she said into his ear.

At that very moment when she could have revealed her secrets, Jillian chose silence. Or possibly in that weird mysterious way that destiny worked, it chose her. There was no need for emails, further dates or explanations. Everything that needed to be said was being said now.

"Goodbye," she whispered and after looking at him one last time, Jillian turned and walked out of the terminal. She didn't look back.

ACKNOWLEDGEMENTS

THANK YOU TO my editor, Nii Parkes at flipped eye, whose faith never wavers. Thanks to Amane Kaneko for the fabulous cover art and to Katie Morris and Robert Koster for your copyediting. Special shout-out to the WOTEs: Mihaela, Fran and Mariko—your advice and suggestions have been invaluable. To Eva, for inspiring me and for your fabulous way with words. To my readers, who have been so generous with their time. A huge thank you to my family and friends for putting up with my incessant book talk. Last but not least, to David who has read copy indefatigably: without your love and support there would be no book.

Thank you to the following publications where stories from this collection have appeared:

Twenty Songs of Love (Inktears 2011)

Frogman (South of South Anthology 2011)

Don't Eat the Prawn (Writer's Hub 2011)

Keeper of Memory (Statement: Cal State L.A. Literary and Art Magazine, 2012